THE
DEVIL'S
WHISPERS

LUCAS HAULT

TCK PUBLISHING.COM

ISBN:
978-1-63161-174-2

Sign up for Lucas Hault's newsletter at
www.lucashault.com/newsletter

Published by TCK Publishing
www.TCKpublishing.com

Get discounts and special deals on our best selling books at
www.TCKpublishing.com/bookdeals

Check out additional discounts for bulk orders at
www.TCKpublishing.com/bulk-book-orders

"I do not wish women to have power over men;
but over themselves."

— **Mary Shelley**

Foreword

December 13, 1919

To His Eminence the Archbishop of Canterbury:

I lie here on my deathbed with a terrible secret, one that hangs heavily upon my heart and belongs locked away in the archives of the Vatican. I must confide in you this secret, Archbishop, for the very fate of the world may depend on it.

Contained in these pages is a collection of journal entries and letters exposing an evil that must never again rise from the shadows of the night. I speak not of vampires or werewolves or goblins of lore, but of something far more sinister.

Take heed of my warning, Archbishop, and read these pages carefully. You hold in your hands the only copy of this manuscript, and though it may be difficult to believe, many people have died in attempting to thwart this evil. I beg of you, Archbishop, to read these pages in earnest, so that their sacrifice will not be in vain.

May God bless and keep you, and may this evil remain forever locked in Hell.

If not, may God have mercy on all of us.

Your servant in life and death,

Father Malcolm Isaac Simpson

1

Gerard Woodward's Journal

February 25th, 1903. Cardiff

I have finally arrived at the hotel after an hour's delay. The cart became stuck in circumstances I comprehend not, and all I could make out through the curtains was the uneven track that had reduced our pace.

I tried talking to the driver, but he was the most ludicrous man I've ever met. He was a stringy fellow, with long hands, a crooked nose, and a terrible scar that marred his cheek and disturbed the oval shape of his face that ended in a long, shaggy beard. He kept adjusting his hat to veil his face, but occasionally I saw his cunning eyes shining under the silver of the moonlight. It gave me a sense of unease, and to overcome the anxiety that had already begun to get the better of me, I tried talking to him in the friendliest manner possible.

But to my amazement, he spoke only nonsense.

For instance, I asked his name and he replied by telling me the story of a girl he once loved in Aberdeen. I sighed, surrendered, and succumbed to his idiocy. He dropped me some distance before the hotel and vanished into the mist.

It was a short walk to the hotel. At the reception desk, I was introduced to a middle-aged woman, plainly but neatly dressed, with a bright, quick face, freckled like a plover's egg.

"Can I help you, sir?" she asked politely. Only through her grinding accent could I make out that she was Irish.

"I need a place somewhere in the hall," I said. "It is only for a couple of hours until Lord Mathers' cart arrives to pick me up."

"May I know your name, good sir?"

"Gerard Woodward."

I noticed a drift in her features, as if she knew about my arrival ahead of time. A drastic change came over her, and I looked about her anxiously in the glare of the lamp. Her face was pale and her eyes heavy, like those of someone who is weighed down by some great anxiety.

"Mr. Woodward, of course," she began. "I have heard so much about the great European lawyer. I never thought I would meet such a revered man. I'm Carla."

I shook my head. "I'm not revered. I just try to be as fair as I can be in my profession."

We were interrupted by the footsteps of a young man who walked behind the table and stood beside Carla. He was well-groomed and trimly clad, with refinement and delicacy in his bearing. He whispered something in Carla's ear, she excused herself, and they retired. A waiter led me to the hall and retreated to the refreshment bar to pour me some drink. I laid my polished stick beside me and settled comfortably on the sofa.

It is a long wait, hence I'm writing in this journal for you, my dearest Raelyn. I apologize for not listening to you, but I was left with no other choice.

It is my profession, my darling. I know you did not wish to see me depart, but I see no harm in visiting a royal old man on his deathbed, a man who wishes to make final provisions of his ancestral estate for his children.

Lord Ferdinand Elvin Mathers is a famous name in Europe, and his royal bloodline is no secret to the world either. To be very honest, I'm eager to visit his inherited castle, where the old man is about to breathe his last. It breaks my heart to have learned how his wife died during childbirth decades ago. Fortunately, the child survived and must be the dearest person in Lord Mathers' life. I think I know what the change in the provisions might be, but who can guess what turn it might take once the declaration is made?

But it is not our problem, Raelyn, and I promise I shall return to London very shortly.

And now I need a nap, for I don't know how long I will have to remain bolted inside the cart. There is presently no task in hand, and I take this as a perfect opportunity to get some rest. I shall write again once I'm away from this place.

I have said it time and again, but I always mean it. I honestly and wholeheartedly love you, Raelyn.

Now, time to doze.

Started from the hotel with bags under my eyes. My nap was not at all satisfying.

The strange cart driver has returned to take me to my destination. What disturbs me most is the prolonged silence between us, for no conversation can be established with such a lunatic. But I am left with no other option. Also, I lack time, as my client is a man of extreme age who could pass away at any moment.

The wind is refreshing; I hear it humming a song of melody across the marshes. The passing of misty boundaries, crags towering on the horizon, and the whining of horses indicates the speed at which we are advancing towards the castle.

After a short distance, I feel the track elevating. Before me lay a green, sloping land of dense trees and thickets. In and out amongst these green hills runs the road, losing itself as it sweeps 'round the grassy curve, or is dominated by the straggling ends of pine woods, which run down the hillsides like tongues of flame. The cart takes a sharp turn through the drift, and here I notice the shining blue of a small river crawling far beneath the cart.

The ride becomes maniacal, for I can feel a continuous jerk, my body swinging to and fro like the pendulum of a grandfather clock. The cart then takes a straight path, and here the road is rugged, but still we seem to fly over it with feverish haste.

The cart comes to an abrupt halt. It seems we have arrived.

I shall write more tonight.

What a place this is, Raelyn.

When we arrived, the moon was staring down from above the clouds, and the world bathed in silver was such a relief to my heart. I peeped through the drapes to study the broad landscape. Beyond the green swelling hills of the land rose mighty slopes of forest up to the lofty steeps. The track stretched a very far extent, bordered with the glorious greens and browns where grass and rock mingle. There was an atmosphere of absolute calm, which momentarily made me forget my worries, or better, my purpose for visiting this part of Cardiff.

I was examining my surroundings when suddenly

(and appallingly, I might add), there appeared a pair of baleful eyes on the other side of the glass. It happened so quickly that I was left aghast like a small child, and it took some time for my nerves to stabilize and for me to realize that it was the cart driver standing before me.

"I'll be right back," said he, teeth shining like ivory. "Do not leave the cart at any expense, y'hear?" The cart driver rubbed his gloved hands pompously and disappeared somewhere around the slope.

It was more than twenty minutes since his departure and still, I saw no sign of him. My anxiety took hold.

I stepped out of the cart and found myself lost in an enormous land that was dead silent, save for the rustling trees of the forest to my right, and the horses that stood motionless behind me, like sculptures of clay. The moving of their jaws was the only sign of life that breathed in them.

There was something sinister in the air, the pines whispering silent threats I could fathom not. For the first time, I regretted not listening to you, Raelyn. I decided to look for the cart driver at once, and was advancing towards the slope when an unusual movement grasped my attention, striking a chill into my heart.

I do not know if it was an illusion or a mere spectre of my startled imagination, but I caught a glimpse of a woman. She was an extraordinarily beautiful woman, very fair and slender, with long blonde hair waving in the breeze and a face as bright as the moon.

I know it isn't appropriate to discuss her flawless beauty, as some day your eyes shall meet this journal, my dearest Raelyn, but it is the truth, which I shall never conceal from you. To be very honest with myself, and with you, I must confess that I was drawn to this mysterious woman lurking in the woods, drawn to her like a butterfly to nectar.

Suddenly, the woman disappeared into the trees.

With a heavy heart and an obstinate mind, I penetrated the woods. Amidst the golden green of the ferny floor and the thorny bushes that scratched at my shoes, I came upon a large, clear pond. The rippling surface was washed in the silver of the full moon. I felt my heart soften over the view before my eyes, which I believe few shall ever be privileged to perceive.

Then, something strange happened. I heard the cry of a toddler—yes, a toddler. I used my stick to clear a path through the bushes, searching in every direction to find the poor child. But I found no one—neither the child nor the woman who, with just a single glance, had beckoned me away from the place I was ordered not to abandon. The child's cry was gone, and all I could hear was a prolonged silence that chilled me to the marrow.

I decided to head straight back to the cart, but before I could make a move, I was grasped by a pair of strong hands.

"Didn't I tell you not to leave the cart?!" cried the cart driver, dragging me out of the woods and pushing me back into the carriage. "You are fortunate that I found you before the evil did."

"What evil?" I asked, panting.

"Aye, you wouldn't believe me even if I told you. But trust me, sir, there is an evil here." I noticed a slight change in his tone, and his glaring eyes softened to a dull frown. "Now, be a good guest and relay nothing of which I say."

He slammed the door right in my face, and our journey resumed.

A weariness descended upon me, and my eyes eventually closed. I have no idea how long I slept, but I awoke when the cart suddenly stopped and the cart driver swung open the door.

As I got out, I noticed dark, rolling clouds overhead and heard the heavy, oppressive zeal of thunder.

And there it was . . .

The gigantic castle stood outlined in the gloom, bearing resemblance to some great fortress of darkness.

A lean, ferret-like man waited for me upon the lowered gate of the castle, wearing a light brown dustcoat and leather leggings, which he wore perhaps in deference to his rustic surroundings. The heavy wooden gate acted as a bridge between the edifice and the rocky surface where I currently stood. I didn't know what was beneath it, perhaps a river or a lowland, but whatever it must be, the spot where I stood seemed to be at a considerable elevation.

"You are desperately awaited, Mr. Woodward," said the ferret man, and after securing the heavy gate, he led me into the entrance hall. I followed him beneath a set of arched stairways and into a row of chambers that wound and swirled like a perpetual maze. He paced the walkway swiftly, eagerly, with a lamp held in his hand and his head sunken upon his chest.

I tried talking to him but each time, he dismissed the conversation with an involuntary nod.

Finally, I was shown into a well-lit chamber, large and ornately decorated, with a gaping fireplace in one corner and a small bookshelf in the other. A pair of windows opened to the inner wing of the castle, while a table beside the cushioned bed was occupied with scrolls.

Stretched upon the bed and surrounded by two people—one a large and terrifying man and the other a young woman—I saw an old man with a large face seated with a thousand wrinkles burned yellow with jaundice. His deep, bile-shot eyes and his high, thin, fleshless nose gave him the resemblance of a fierce, ancient bird of prey.

It was my client—the royal old man, Lord Ferdinand Elvin Mathers, breathing his last. I noticed a ray of delight in his feeble eyes at my arrival. He waved a quivering hand towards me. I quickly adjusted myself on a chair beside his bed, and the old man, in a shuddering voice, began whispering into my ear. I raised my gaze to look at the three people around us who, quite eagerly and impatiently, stood with folded arms and muted breath.

"Remember what I've said, Mr. Woodward," he concluded. "It is now your responsibility to ensure that all my property is distributed between my children exactly in the proportion I've described."

The proportion, as whispered to me by Lord Mathers, was to be distributed in three parts. He was leaving behind two children—a son and a daughter. The largest portion would be inherited by his younger daughter, who I already assumed was dearest to the old man. The second portion would be taken by his elder son. The small portion that remained would be distributed equally among the poor folk who had pledged their lives in service of the castle.

There was no sign of Lord Mathers' son in the room, but I was promptly introduced to his daughter—Helena Mathers, the epitome of beauty, with hair the color of chestnut, dressed in the perfect manner of a highborn.

Standing opposite her was the large, horrifically scarred man who introduced himself as Jared, the butler. He was ghastly to look upon, with a slinking gait and a sidelong glance that seemed charged with malice. Each time I looked at him, I felt a shiver run down my spine.

"I'll escort you to your chamber, Mr. Woodward,"

proposed Maverick, the ferret man who had initially led me into the room. "Dinner will be waiting on your table."

I rose from my seat and looked at the old man, who feverishly groaned and kept his gaze fixed on his daughter, who perhaps brought a sense of relief to his fragile state during this most crucial time. Heavy marks of distress hung upon Helena's face, watching her father slipping steadily into the arms of death.

But what captured my attention was the butler, for Jared suddenly shifted his glance from the window to the shelves, and then back to the old man upon his deathbed. I noticed a flicker of terror upon his face which he tried in his best way to conceal, and which also gave rise to my suspicion.

"I shall return tomorrow, My Lord," I said.

I was then led to my room somewhere in the far north of the castle, and I knew I would be hard-pressed to find my way fruitfully to Mr. Mathers' chamber on my own. As I mentioned before, the numerous corridors are like some great labyrinth, dominated by similar doors and a gloom that binds the place together like a ghostly trap, especially for newcomers like me.

My room was plainly furnished with a modest camp-bed, a small wooden shelf full of books, an armchair against the wall, a round table, and a large iron safe. A hot meal waited for me on the table. Dinner was delicious, though I felt weary and needed to rest.

My worries could wait until morning.

February 26th, 1903

I slept heartily and now my body feels relieved. I see departing rays of sunlight outside my window, and the approach of evening strikes me with exasperation, for never in my entire life have I slept so profoundly. Rising at such a time of day makes me feel as if I have been resurrected to face the day of judgement.

I try the doorknob, but the room is strangely locked from the outside. I pound on the door and yell for someone to let me out. I wait, but I am met with silence. I suddenly feel like a prisoner. What chills my heart most is the fact that someone came into my room whilst I slept, evidenced by the steaming meal resting on my table. Fish, bread, and a bowl of soup. It must have been Maverick, but why must he lock me in? Is there something here I must not see?

The thought troubles me.

Again, I regret not listening to you, Raelyn. I pray I'm allowed to leave this place within a few hours. The purpose for my visit to Mr. Mathers' castle has been fulfilled. I have been made aware of the proportions of his estate, and I plan to part on good terms with the old man as soon as I am escorted back to his chamber.

Dusk is about to concede to the invincible darkness which dominates this place, and still there is no one around to help me out of my chamber. There is something abominable about this place; I can feel it in my bones.

I have nothing else to occupy my time right now, and so, I'm writing. I love to write, but at this moment I'm afraid. At this moment, my writing is not out of passion, but because of the terror and anxiety that this place has unleashed upon me.

There is a horrible stillness which stifles this place, and it makes me feel like I'm the only individual alive.

Tonight, I tried peering out of the window in order to study this part of the castle as minutely as possible, but in vain.

My eyes then shifted to the iron safe. At first it felt rude, also impudent, but having absolutely no other thing to distract my curiosity, I set foot towards the safe. The Matherses are the wealthiest creatures in Cardiff, so I imagined the safe was full of gems or gold. But before I could lay my quivering hands upon the cold steel, the door flung open.

To my surprise, in rushed the old man's daughter, Helena, with a lamp held in her hand and tears in her eyes.

"Is everything all right?" I asked.

"You have been summoned," she replied. "Father wants to see you one last time."

Intent on leaving, I began to gather my belongings when she threw a fierce glance at me.

"It can wait," she said, half annoyed. I gave an apologetic nod and joined her in the corridors. This time, I was careful in navigating the passages we walked. We crossed a long corridor, took a right, a left, and again a right, and descended a flight of stairs before following the familiar passage that ended at Lord Mathers' room.

The old man was deathly pale on his bed, eyes aghast in horror. I settled beside his bed, followed by his daughter, who dropped into a chair beside me. Lord Mathers had become remarkably weak over the past few hours, for his lips quivered terribly as he tried to speak. But the poor man lacked the strength to force out even a single word from his narrowed mouth, and in turn, he held his daughter's hand and placed it upon my palm.

I know it hurts you to read it, my sweet Raelyn, but I was momentarily struck with fantasy. I turned my glance towards the lady, stagnant by the sorrow of her dying father and staring constantly at him. I saw for the first time since my arrival that the distorted features of Lord Ferdinand Elvin Mathers had relaxed, and there flickered a ray of hope in his horror-stricken eyes.

"It is your responsibility now . . . to take good care of her," muttered the old man at last. And then, he retired. I believed him to have finally passed away, but then his shallow breathing and weak groans made it manifest that his soul was still trapped within that feeble body. I left the old man undisturbed and walked back into the labyrinth towards my quarters.

Helena followed at my heels.

"I apologize if my father has offended you in any way," said she. "He's a man in delirium and his words shouldn't be taken too seriously."

"No apologies necessary," I said.

She placed her lamp on the table and sank into a chair beside me. Even amid the impending tragedy of her father, we talked. For a moment, I almost forgot I was speaking with a stranger. Helena's charm intensified each time she opened her mouth to speak.

And suddenly, I stopped and I stared. The hair on my arms stood on end.

Helena's fair beauty, in some way, reminded me of the mysterious woman I saw in the woods. The fascinating creature had been much too far from my sight and so I failed to study her face, but her overall appearance was as remarkable as that of Helena's. It was only the varying colour of their hair which allowed me to remain calm. Helena's was chestnut brown; the woman in the woods was blonde.

Helena spoke about her formal education, her stay in

the south, and her meeting with George Mooney, the man she intended to marry. Mooney, she said, planned to move to Cardiff, and after her father's death, they would start a new life together. She then reassured me that I would no longer be forced to stay at the castle once her father passed away.

I do not know what not to believe, but as it stands, I feel trapped. Everything around me appears to be a beautiful lie.

Helena stood and walked to the door with an innocent smile, though I noticed a swift darkness in her eyes. Before leaving, she spoke of Maverick who would soon return with my dinner, and then as usual, I was locked inside. Again, I pounded my fists on the thick oaken door and demanded Lady Helena to unlock it. But there was no response.

Why must I always be locked in? Am I a guest or a damned prisoner?

The thought chills me.

I do not know what to believe.

2

Gerard Woodward's Journal, Continued

February 27th, 1903

It was around dawn when I woke up breathless, as if something had been choking me to death. There was no intruder in my room, and yet my heart trembled over the fear that I was being watched.

I feel as if something lurks in the dark, a shadow that has been my constant companion ever since I've stepped foot inside this hell. To prove my point, I shall relate another event that took place last night:

I waited much too long for my dinner, but there was still no sign of Maverick or Jared, the butler. I felt defeated over the extreme silence of the place. And as by the universal law of psychology, nothingness gave rise to curiosity . . .

The safe, standing across from my bed, captured my attention.

I sighed and snuck towards the safe, careful all the while not to make a sound. As I reached the spot and was about to lay my hands over the lock, the door swung open thunderously and Maverick entered with a tray full of fish. I cannot help wondering if his well-timed entrance was but a mere coincidence. What brings horror to my heart is the fact that I heard no footsteps. I'm sure of it. I heard no sound—not a single click of his boot.

When he departed with a bow, I heard the telltale lock of the door and was unable to fall back asleep. I abandoned my efforts to open the safe, as I feared Maverick or some other inhabitant of the castle might interrupt me again.

Having lost my appetite, I began to examine the room, wishing to find a way to escape my confines so that I might further explore this wing of the castle (and perhaps, find a way out).

I moved to the window and observed it very minutely. My heart raced, but it was my only option. I peered down thoroughly across the window frame, and I found a narrow row of stone slabs protruding out from the castle's exterior walls, at the base of each window. Intense anticipation overtook me. I found I could finally breathe in some relief, but the peril of my plan never slipped from my mind.

With cold skin and shallow breath, I hoisted myself up the windowpane, crossed my leg across the frame, and stepped onto the slab, finding my balance before finally making my move. I held the window frame for support, and very steadily shuffled across to the next slab. I thrice repeated my course of action, and with a stiff support against the wall, made my chase towards the exterior of a new room, the window already wide open.

I got hold of the frame and hoisted myself inside.

The chamber seemed ancient, completely dark and occupied by a very foul smell that burned my nostrils. The stench was unbearable, and fortunately, I found the door leading out of the chamber unlocked. I walked out into the corridor and gasped in the fresh air.

The long hallway was pitch black, and I couldn't help imagining the sinister features of Jared, the butler, skulking through the shadows.

I may not be properly judging the man. We have only

shared a brief, single encounter, but I find something peculiar about him. I confess I take a good measure of interest in writing about Helena, but remembering Jared is far more frightening.

My wandering, misty imagination was suddenly broken by a loud clanging noise that echoed from one of the neighbouring chambers. My nerves tingled, and I suddenly imagined some sad soul chained inside one of the rooms.

I took a deep breath and moved in the direction of the sound, which grew louder and louder as I approached a new door. As I grasped the doorknob, my mind wanted to rebel, but the obstinate whispers of the devil led me onward. I held my breath, and with compressed eyes and a thumping heart, I pushed open the door.

A cold breeze wafted upon my face, blowing my hair and chilling my flesh. As my eyes adjusted, I was hit by a sudden paroxysm of fear, gaping in absolute terror at the sight of a beastly figure fleeing out of the window. It dashed away quicker than a lizard on the wall. Whatever it was, I succeeded in securing a rapid glance at it against the fading silver of the sky and found a heavy chain hanging around its body.

My boots seemed bolted to the floor. I wanted to flee away immediately, but then similar footsteps fell upon my ears, and I rushed to shut the door. Through the small cracks in the wood, I saw the passing of a figure holding a lamp; I assumed it was Jared. The lamp's soft, passing light momentarily tore the gloom inside the room, and I was awestruck at discovering another safe fixed at one corner of the chamber, similar to the safe in my own room.

Though I was tempted to try opening this safe, I rather feared the idea of Jared opening the door to my room and finding me gone. And so, I impotently dragged myself out of the chamber, back out onto the exterior ledge, and carefully scaled my way back into my room.

The sky was dull, while darkness had begun to dissolve over the rising sunbeams in the far horizon. For me it was a sign of relief. I stretched myself over the bed, gazing at the wonderful sky all the time as my eyelids drooped, and that is where I remember I was lost in sleep.

Waking up was exceptionally abhorrent.

When I opened my eyes, I saw Helena leaning towards me, washed in the yellow glimmer of the flickering lamp. I felt the rush of her warm breath tickling my cheek. At first, I was unnerved, but then I felt somewhat soothed at the sight of such a mesmerizing woman crouched beside me. I felt almost bewitched. Looking out the window, I realized that morning had yet not approached, as outside it was still dark.

"Is there anything you would like to share?" she asked, straightening her back once she realized I was awake.

I shook my head vigorously.

"Really?" she asked, staring at me with dubious eyes and a soft smile.

"I don't know what you're speaking of, my good lady."

I must have sounded dull or hesitant, for she frowned at my response. Her smile returned, but hardened. As she glared down at me, the flickering shadows of the lamp made her beautiful features appear almost demonic. She muttered something under her breath which sounded curiously like some sort of curse. I was perplexed, for as she rose with the lamp, I observed a varying tinct in her eyes and a yellowish hue stretching across her pale face. Initially, I assumed the flame of her lamp to be the reason for her sickly pallor, but even as she lowered the lamp, the pallor remained.

She then disappeared out the door.

I have observed this place and these people for some time now. They so enjoy the darkness of the castle and so, I concluded that it was the coming of daylight that forced Helena to take her departure.

I waited for my breakfast, but Maverick never arrived. He seemed to vanish into the walls like the other inhabitants of this hellish edifice. Around noon, I made up my mind to try the safe again. I was certain I would be interrupted, but surprisingly, no one barged into my room as I tried unlocking the safe. It was perfectly sealed and secured. I tried a few more lofty tricks, but to no avail.

I climbed out the window as I had the night before, scaled the exterior wall, landed into the adjoining room, and stepped out into the corridor. The castle was silent and lifeless. With subdued terror in my heart, I walked to the door where I encountered the strange creature in the dark. My hands still felt weak, but I pushed open the door only to find the chamber completely empty, save for the other large safe fixed in the corner.

I don't know why, but I smiled when my hands reached for the safe—perhaps my fortune was finally returning, or perhaps I was slowly losing my mind. I thought of Helena Mathers, her beautiful and deadly face, the fury she might show if she ever caught me. And yet, my own stubbornness got the better of me, for I had finally decided to break out of this prison and return to London, where you desperately await my return, Raelyn.

The safe in this room wasn't locked, and as I pulled it open, my eyes rested upon what looked like an ancient vase. Glittering golden script carved over its violet body gave it a somewhat sacred form. The pottery itself, along with the imperial font used in its inscription, reflected the brilliant art that might have been in practice once upon a time.

I was so involved in examining the artifact that I barely noticed the pair of keen yellow eyes watching me from a nearby corner. A ferocious black cat leaned against the door in a position to prey upon me. I tried to hush it away, but I only irritated it further. The cat pounced and I dodged, watching the animal fly above my head, where it briskly collided with the wall and escaped through the open window.

Even the house pets keep close watch on me! Nowhere is safe.

I placed the vase back into the safe, closed it, and slid back into the corridor. I desired to peek into each room, regardless of the time it would consume, for I had the whole day at hand.

I started my investigation with the clear objective of finding my way out of the castle. The wide passages were clean and tiled, with unplastered walls showcasing large, stacked boulders—yet another brilliant art form of bygone architecture. As I swept along the corridors, I noticed the entangling beauty of the castle in the warm sunlight, an ethereal view I'd not yet seen. I saw stark slate roofs through the windows and great, green blotches of parched lichen upon the gray walls, grown in such perfect fashion that it gave a unique imprint, as if by the architecture itself.

I moved through the stairwell and landed somewhere near Lord Mathers' chamber. I had grown more rigid in my purpose, my head held high in fortitude, my courage risen, for I was about to enter the old man's room and part ways with him. No obstacle could block my path, not even the payment I had not yet received for my services.

As I entered his room, I saw Lord Ferdinand Elvin Mathers lying stagnant in his bed. He was very pale, fragile, and was silently buried in thought. He had a pained expression upon his white and fearful face.

"Lord Mathers!" I called. "Are you alright?"

There was no rest for him, no peace, no way to forget his deathly state; turn where he might, there also was that cunning, grinning face at his elbow known as Fate. Death can be frightening—this I can confirm by the recent incidents that have plagued me whilst I've been here. I wanted to narrate the entire chain of events of my stay to the lord of the house, but in looking at his horrible state, I held my tongue.

Lord Mathers suddenly grabbed my hands, his palms as cold as ice. He moved his quivering lips to try and say something, but then a deathly pallor spread over his face and his eyes became fixed on a single point, motionless and terrified. I followed his gaze to the door and discovered what had instantly paralyzed the old man.

I shuddered at the sight of Jared, the butler, standing at the door. Though he grinned, there was a malevolence in his posture, his eyes staring like those of a fox.

"You aren't supposed to leave your room, Sir," he said. "It is not the polite manner of a gentleman to wander about the castle on one's own."

"Who is taking care of Lord Mathers?" I asked, annoyed. His rat-like face and impolite manners had left me in utmost exasperation. "You aren't supposed to leave him on his own."

"I do nothing of my own consent, Sir. It was Miss Helena who ordered me to clean the dungeons. The maid never showed up for work."

I did not believe him.

"I see you are troubled, Sir," he said, and his face seemed to redden with the effort with which he tried to compress his malicious grin. "I shall accompany you back to your room."

"But Lord Mathers—"

"I shall attend to him. Come. Shan't let your lunch get cold," he said. "Now."

I took a deep breath and held back my agitation. And like a man heading to his own execution, I followed the rigid butler back to my room.

3

Gerard Woodward's Journal, Continued

February 28th, 1903

I have just been awoken by a terrible scream. It chills my heart, and I know in my bones that someone has been severely hurt, or perhaps killed.

Once again, I curse my decision for not listening to you, my beloved Raelyn, and for so gladly diving into this hell of a castle. It is some hours before midnight, and as usual, I'm locked inside my room. What hidden purpose there is behind my imprisonment I can fathom not. I feel there are things going on around here, dire things that I can't even begin to imagine.

At times, I feel as if everything is a trap and that I am the bait.

I honestly don't know if we will ever meet again, my dearest Raelyn, but I need to act. If death is my only option, I need to unveil the truth that has brought me before it.

March 1st, 1903

This may be my final entry, but what I have come across needs to be mentioned. Somehow, I will find a way to get this journal into your hands, Raelyn. It will be your responsibility then to disclose this truth to others.

Last night, the prolonged scream shattered my nerves, and there was absolutely no way I would overlook such a dilemma. I knew I was not mistaken. It was no delusion.

I fell back into my perilous path along the exterior of the window, through to the adjoining room, and was shortly within the corridor. I checked some of the other rooms at random, only to find them empty or locked, as expected.

But then came a distraction in the form of an approaching light, a light I instantly recognized. It was the same fellow who had crossed the corridor the other night, when I encountered the hellish creature in one of these dusty rooms. The burning light threw a feeble shadow against the wall, and I found no difficulty in deducing it to be none other than the wicked butler.

Jared was coming my way.

I immediately slinked into one of the rooms. With muted breath and my heart pounding in my chest, I watched the man cross the corridor, his face restless and haggard. I noticed the lamp in his hand shake as he shivered, though it seemed out of fear rather than the cold. I quietly slid out into the passage, using the darkness to my advantage, and I followed the butler, cautious enough to maintain my distance.

He strode down the wide, labyrinthine corridors and down the arched stairway, until finally we were outside beneath a lurid sky. I noticed his manners growing more hesitant, and he kept turning around to ensure he wasn't being followed. I was careful all the while, and despite maintaining the gap, I made sure not to lose sight of him.

For a moment, Jared stopped, his breath fogging in the night. To his left, I saw the enormous gate of the castle through which I had entered this purgatory.

Freedom at last, barred by a massive iron lock.

To his right was a semi-circular structure I remembered seeing upon my arrival. It was separated from the rest of the grounds by a vast, green garden, a canopy of dense trees, and a spongy carpet of moss and clovers. Bordered around the edges and scattered around the corners were trimmed bushes, with blooming flowers of jasmine and rose. There were granite slabs spread amidst the elegant garden, and a large fountain beside the trees.

Jared wiped his forehead with the sleeve of his coat and resumed his walk toward the stone structure. I crouched behind the bushes and continued my pursuit. He proceeded to a set of stairs and descended into the bowels of the structure, presumably into the dungeons.

As I followed, I was hit by a very unpleasant smell, the odour of lime mixed with blood and flesh. I choked, and it only got stronger as I descended into the darkness.

I doubted if I would ever return to the surface, but obstinacy and curiosity got the better of me, as so often happens. I firmly believed that if I followed Jared, all my questions about this hellish castle would be answered, and placing my handkerchief against my nose, I followed him downward into the darkness. Dimly lit torches were sconced to the walls, throwing flickering light upon the damp stone floor below. Upon the flagstones, I noticed engraved scriptures that looked like some religious text.

I watched Jared rush across the dungeon and enter a nearby chamber. I followed, and as I settled within the shadows of the chamber's entrance, I felt the blood leave my face entirely, for the sudden weeping of an infant shook the very depths of my soul.

I saw Helena standing in the corner, though it couldn't be Helena, for this woman's hair was blonde, not brown. All other features were exactly the same: the porcelain skin, the mesmeric face, the queenly stature, the slim, pointed nose, and even the hues of her eyes. Save for her hair, this was a perfect replica of Helena Mathers.

This, then, was the mysterious woman from the woods. I was certain of it.

And then, my eyes fell upon another woman who suddenly emerged from the shadows. She was dressed in all black, heavily veiled, and appeared in a considerable state of excitement. She held two newborn babes in her arms. Was this the elusive maid that Jared had earlier mentioned?

Jared moved into place beside her, and both servants bowed their heads before the aristocratic woman.

The woman from the woods addressed them both in whispers, and the maid raised her veil as she spoke. I could see that the poor lady was indeed in a pitiable state of agitation, her face drawn and gray, with restless and frightened eyes, like those of some hunted animal. I guessed her to be a woman of thirty or so, though her hair was shot with premature gray, her expression weary and haggard. Jared shared a similar agitation.

I had no idea what this secret liaison was all about, but it was clear to me that both servants thoroughly feared this perfect replica of Lady Helena.

The woman took one of the infants in her fair hands and kissed it. The other remained with the maid, who proceeded with the butler to sit at a pew. The woman suddenly approached the corridor where I secretly stood, and I swept back to the wall, away from the flickering light and into a corner shrouded in humid mist. I was hit yet again by the sharp odour, the cause of which I had still not discovered. I stood concealed and watched as she entered the corridor and walked right past me.

I followed her with my eyes, then chased her like a shadow, watching her proceed towards the uneven stairs. Here I noticed a secret chamber adjoined to the stairwell, separated with a massive door of rusted iron. I followed the woman and watched her slip into the room, the infant still whimpering in her arms.

I took a deep, harrowing breath, and when I entered the room, I found no sign of the woman or the child, as if they had vanished into thin air.

I was maddened by both frustration and intrigue. It all seemed like a horrible nightmare to me, and I expected that I should suddenly awake and find myself locked away in my chamber. I rubbed my eyes and pinched myself to see if I was awake, and my flesh answered.

I was indeed awake.

I scanned every corner of the empty room but in vain, for there was nothing to be discovered, save for another safe fixed in the corner, much like the one in my own room and the one where I had discovered the ancient vase. I no longer possessed the courage to stay in this room or to open the safe and disclose whatever it comprised. I guessed that it held some other useless bit of pottery, and that itself was enough to silence the devil's whispers in my head.

I emerged up the stairs and into the vast garden, where I caught a glimpse of a dark figure loitering far from my sight and beside the large, locked gate. I felt tranquilized, as though I was being watched, or perhaps stalked. I turned around to peer into the dungeons, and fortunately, I saw no stalker lurking in the shadows.

I crawled amongst the bushes, and upon reaching the end of the garden, I saw Maverick pacing the path at the base of the gate. He appeared in a state of intense agitation, as if struck with catastrophe. I watched him for a moment, and as he turned his back to me, I snuck back into the castle.

I followed the familiar, dingy corridors and found myself at the old man's door. I peered through a crack in the wood. Inside the dimly lit chamber, I saw the real Helena Mathers seated grimly beside her father, her chestnut hair cascading down her back. For a moment, I studied her features and affirmed with full confidence that I was not wrong. This was not the same woman from the dungeons.

I wanted to join Lady Helena and inquire about the mystifying damsel of the dark, whom I strongly suspect to be her twin. But I was helpless. I had no idea what fresh trouble I would land myself into if I dared to interrupt Helena's grief.

I surrendered to the unveiled mystery and proceeded instead towards the other end of the passage. I found another set of stairs, followed them higher and higher, and wondered if these stairs might grant me access to the roof. As I climbed, pride and hope grew within me. I rejoiced over the fact that I would no longer be confined within the four walls of this fortress of hell. I breathed in the air of deliverance, but I did not let the temporary merriment chain me in my delusions.

It couldn't be denied that despite finding a way out of the labyrinth, I was still locked inside the cage. This magnificent castle is still a prison, and I am the prisoner.

I pushed upward through a trapdoor and clambered up into the night air. My arrival on the roof was both startling and impetus, for as I arrived at the top, a heavy cloud passed across the face of the crescent moon, so that I was left in pitch blackness. The moonbeam returned shortly thereafter, but between the rapid interval of dark and light, I perceived a pair of bright and savage yellow eyes glaring at me from the shadows.

And then, as quickly as I'd seen them, the eyes were gone.

I began to feel some nocturnal presence weighing heavily upon me. I shivered in every limb—not because of the cold, for it was the least of my worries, but because of the recent dark events that had begun to devour the life inside of me. I became afraid of my own shadow, and my brain swirled with all sorts of horrible imaginings. I realized the seriousness of my condition and how appallingly I was trapped, for my legs felt weak as I examined my vast surroundings.

I held myself firmly against the battlements and peered over the side. The castle stretched over a cliff at an enormous height, with only a single exit through the gigantic, padlocked gate on the narrow roadway below. The remaining sides of the cliff disappeared into what seemed like the profound depths of hell. I could not properly guess as to what lay so far below; perhaps a great flowing river or sharp rocks set as a trap to dissuade intruders from approaching the old castle.

I fear I have been terribly wrong in imagining any method of escape. I have a vile feeling growing in my heart that I'm exactly where the devil wants me to be.

March 2nd, 1903

It happened while I was asleep. I swear it upon all I hold sacred that never have I experienced so real a dream in my entire life.

I saw in my dream a very beautiful and imperial garden, blooming with mesmerizing flowers of all colours and fragrances. It was a smell that I could breathe in as I lay hypnotized in slumber. A full moon crowned over the cloudless sky, its reflection like a shimmering diamond over a large, freshwater loch.

A narrow, convex bridge of fine wood stretched across the loch, upon which I pursued a voice so melodious and enchanting that it tugged me along stronger than a magnet to iron. A portion of the loch glittered with floating water lilies, resembling the allure of fireflies floating in darkness. I also saw a pony on the other side of the bridge, chewing the grass of the ferny floor.

A ravishing view it was, which grew all the more inviting as I proceeded.

On reaching the other side of the bridge, I entered a blissful garden. My eyes beheld a feminine figure clad in a dressing gown of pure silk. She was barefoot and touched her fingers to her long, curly tresses, the colour similar to her faded yellow gown. She sat upon a rectangular crag of rock and hummed the melancholy song I had followed. She began gently brushing her hair with a mystical comb woven from sun or moonbeams, for it glittered with a divine light, the rays of which trickled over her smooth skin like droplets of milk over butter.

For a moment, I was drawn to her by both fantasy and fear, as a single glance at this enticing creature had stunned me into what I might call a beautiful death. An absurd fright took hold of me as she suddenly ended her song. I stood breathless, watching as she turned a sidelong glance at me.

The woman said nothing, but through the dark shroud covering her face, I noticed a yellow gleam in her eyes.

She offered me a rose and then held my hand. My heart beat dreadfully, for the strength with which she grasped my palm was enormous, far beyond the capability of any man or woman I've ever met. I suddenly felt a heavy weight upon my chest. A sharp stench entered my nose, and I felt something choking my throat.

I awoke with a start.

Imagine my horror, dearest Raelyn, in finding a single rose clutched in my fist.

Startled, I fell off my bed and twisted my ankle in the process. My room stank of the odour I smelled in the dungeons last night. I shivered terribly, as if in a palsy. I felt dizzy and nauseous, my strength drained from my body. There was no one around to help me, and I repeatedly failed to pull myself back into bed.

As usual, I am locked inside my room. I doubt I shall ever successfully escape from this hellish fortress. I shall try with all I have left to get this journal to you by some means, my dearest Raelyn. Forgive me if I break my promise, for it shall only happen if ever I die in this infernal place. If this be my final inscription, I bid you farewell.

I want you to know, Raelyn, that I truly and wholeheartedly love you. You are the only gem of utmost value that I have ever held or possessed, and I apologize for going against your advice regarding my visit to Lord Mathers. I will leave no stone unturned to gather as much information as I can about this place and will continue my struggle until my last breath if there is any hope of my survival.

Do not grieve if these are my last words.

I feel my condition worsen—and now, I rest.

4

Gerard Woodward's Journal, Continued

March 5th, 1903

I am happy to be able to write again. I feel as if a heavy burden has been lifted from me, and I'm well and alive. My condition, my beloved Raelyn, has improved. My ankle still hurts, and I doubt if I will ever have my initial strength back, for my muscles ache when too much effort is placed upon them.

Last night, I tested the efforts of my body . . .

It took me a lot of courage and effort to traverse across the narrow slabs outside the window, and upon dropping into the familiar web of corridors, I noticed they were darker than usual. I suddenly saw looming lights and heard footsteps approaching me from every possible direction. I was helpless, with no possible chance to defend myself against my impending quarries, so vulnerable was I.

I then noticed an ugly door behind my back, a small door that appeared the worse for wear. And so, I snuck behind it and took shelter in what I assumed was a tiny, decrepit closet.

Through the crack in the door, I saw the same mysterious woman from the dungeons stride past and down the corridor. Following at her heels was the maid, chasing her mistress in a most humble manner. They walked past and disappeared into the stairwell, but before

I could make my move to follow them, another figure emerged from the darkness of the maze and followed aimlessly into the stairwell.

I do not know who it was, only that it was a man. I do not know what his purpose was, but looking at him gave me no feeling of comfort. I knew it wasn't Jared or Maverick, for now I recognize their body structures and their individual gaits.

I could not relax from my uncomfortably contorted position within the remarkably confined chamber.

I caught a glimpse of another woman walking with a lamp. The light slid across her face, and I could see that it was Lady Helena, approaching from yet a different corridor. An unnatural thrill ran through me, and I knew I had to follow her. And so, I finally emerged from the tiny chamber, and upon getting a better look at it, I noticed that I had been hiding in an old, upturned coffin.

I escaped my would-be tomb, ran through the shadows, and saw Helena entering a room at the end of the corridor. The distance between us wasn't vast, but by the time I peeped through the door (almost immediately after she walked inside), I was astounded to find an empty chamber.

There was no sign of Helena. She simply vanished, exactly as the mysterious woman had vanished in the dungeons. The similarities and circumstances between the two women had me struggling to acknowledge the fact that they were two entirely different people.

I felt an invisible force with me in the dark, which I feared had its hungry eyes fixed upon me. I could not visually perceive its presence, but still I felt (and continue to feel) the terror that tortured me from my first night in this castle. Trapped in this mesh of menace and illusion,

I felt myself fading under the devil's grip, which made me so weak that, for an instant, I wanted to succumb to my fate.

But then, I thought of you, Raelyn, and an abrupt aggression came over me. Then and there, I made up my mind to finally meet with Lord Mathers, to relay to him my frustrations of being held prisoner, and to also plead before him, if required, to give me passage to leave this strange world of his.

I found his corridor, stopped outside his door, and peeped through the keyhole. To my great astonishment, I saw the old man standing up and leaning against his bed! He no longer appeared to be feeble nor at death's door, but was rather full of strength and life.

I lost my breath. I couldn't move. I couldn't believe the man before my eyes to be Lord Ferdinand Elvin Mathers.

I saw Lady Helena standing before the fireplace, the glimmer of the flames revealing her triumphant, malicious grin.

While I watched Lord Mathers, I became chained in a state of horror, as I suddenly heard footsteps behind me. I struggled to turn around, only to collapse at the sight of the mysterious woman from the dungeons, Lady Helena's replica, standing behind me.

I screamed. And then, darkness.

The next thing I remember is waking up breathless in my bed, drenched in sweat, my body shivering terribly. I still cannot comprehend if it was real or if I was dreaming.

After writing this, I feel my newfound strength suddenly weaken. Heaven knows what is happening to me.

March 8th, 1903

I must relate another incident that shook me violently.

These things always happen in the dark. I have become accustomed to it. I have also grown used to sleeping all day. There is no other thing to do. Besides, I seem to have developed a serious health condition, and I suspect my state is getting worse each day.

Last night, I was shown to Lord Mathers' chamber. I held my head high in fortitude, though still weak in my bones, but I once again found the courage to ask for my departure back to London. I also wanted to emphasize the fact that my service was no longer required, since the old man seemed to be falling to recovery, as I had witnessed firsthand the other night.

However, a terrible shock seized me as I was led in by Maverick. Before my eyes was the same fragile creature whom I had witnessed my first night in the castle. Lord Mathers was again pale and haggard, and resembled the look of a hunted creature whose soul might leave his body at any moment.

I was forced to believe it had all been a dream, for it was the only explanation that made sense.

"I know what brings you here, Mr. Woodward," the old man struggled to say before I could even drop into my seat. "Arrivals demand departures; this I understand. You have someone waiting for you in London; this I know. Your business here is over; this I support. You wish to bid your farewell tonight; this, however, I oppose."

I couldn't believe my ears.

"I propose before you, Lord Mathers, my utmost urgency to return to London. I have unfinished business there to look after. Your hospitality has been highly appreciated, and I shall never hold back if ever I'm called to the service of your family or estate at any time in the future."

This last bit was a lie, one of the first that has left my lips in years.

Lord Mathers remained rigid as Jared, the butler, entered the chamber with a noticeably cunning smile he seemed desperate to conceal.

"Your business and your stay in our castle have been much anticipated," muttered the old man. "Give me two more days, Mr. Woodward, that is all. You shall afterwards be escorted to the gate, regardless of if I live or die. I give you my solemn word."

Two days. That's all I had left to endure. I felt my face glow with delight.

I spoke to the old man about his affairs a while longer, until the servants left and Lady Helena suddenly appeared. There was a little bewilderment in her voice as she spoke, and she endeavored time and again during our talk to inquire about my family.

There was a flicker of merriment in her eyes when she learned that you, my dear Raelyn, are the only family I have. I can only pray that Lady Helena, along with the rest of Lord Mathers' staff, remain confined within the boundaries of this castle.

As I started for my room, an unnatural fear overtook me. I felt as though I was being followed in the dark. The fact that I had grown feeble over the past few days chilled me further, for deep down I knew how easy it would be for someone to overtake me. With an unbearable terror crawling down my spine, I bolted towards my room, using my stick for support all the while. Unfortunately, I took a wrong turn and became lost within the web of corridors.

Suddenly, I stopped. Far in the mist and towards the stairs, I saw a tall figure moving. I followed it onto the roof but found no sign of anyone, save for myself. A cold breeze blew upon my face as I heard the screams of ravens.

I turned to the battlements, and what remained of my strength escaped me. Never had I seen anything more dreadful, more hellish—for I saw, with frozen eyes and somber senses, a shrouded woman inclined over one of the battlements. Her eyes were as furious and yellow as that of a savage beast, and a conspiracy of ravens flapped and squawked all around her. Beneath her shroud protruded locks of golden hair.

It was the woman from my dream. From my nightmare.

Before I could dash away or even scream, the creature was in front of me. I felt strong fists grasping my arms and shaking me violently. It was real, all of it. The horrible woman, the army of ravens, the darkness, the moon, the battlements.

And yet, when I yielded to my attacker, I found myself in my room, hunched over my bed, as if it had all been a dream.

I was dumbfounded.

It was Helena who had awoken me from my delirium, but what hooked my attention was the unusual strength she possessed. I do not know what effect her presence brings upon me or my body, but each time I discover her in my room, I feel my health deteriorate.

She told me that my condition disheartens her and Lord Mathers, and that she cares for me, which I do not believe. I asked about my encounter with Lord Mathers, and she attested his word held firm, that I would be leaving in two days' time. She was simply here to make sure I was all right. She hardly spoke to me once I was awake, and then she retired to the corridor.

Now I must wait for two days, after which I will be set free from this prison, as promised. I don't know if the old man's words will stand true or not, but I trust myself.

All I can do now is wait.

5

Gerard Woodward's Journal, Continued

March 10th, 1903

The day of my departure has finally arrived, per Lord Mathers' promise. There is no one to disturb me in broad daylight, which I shall take as a divine opportunity to complete my crucial errand.

I've made all my preparations accordingly and wait for my time to depart, though I know I won't be released before nightfall. I keep hearing strange voices echoing behind the walls of this accursed castle. I wonder what the fuss is all about. I waited for breakfast a long time, but Maverick never showed up. I presume my hosts are upset, for I believe they aren't pleased with me finally parting ways with them. My heart churns with anticipation, and it beats with a rhythm of delight.

I will finally get to see you, my dearest Raelyn. I don't know how to describe it in words. All I can do is to wait, perhaps for the very last time.

I was starving by the time Jared arrived with lunch. I wanted to ask him about the delay at breakfast, but instead I remained silent at my table. Jared watched in silence whilst I ate and departed as soon as I finished. Evening for me came as a sign of relief, where I could smell the fragrance of freedom in the winds and admire the charm of fading red over the elegant sky.

A deathly silence lay upon the place as I prepared for my departure. Thankfully, Jared had finally left the door unlocked.

Suddenly, a terrible and prolonged cry of unimaginable horror fell upon my ears. I rushed out of my room and followed the horrible yell, and by the time I crossed the threshold of Lord Mathers' chamber, a cold struck through my feeble heart, and I felt it explode beneath my breast.

There was no sign of the old man.

His bed was fresh and empty, as if it had never been used. The flame in the furnace was about to die, and through the last flicker of light, my eyes fell upon the window. I immediately froze and collapsed in terror.

Just outside the window, there in the dark, crouched an ape-like creature, tilting its head to peek into the chamber. It watched me and quietly bared its teeth, then growled and eventually disappeared in the mist.

I was left pale and shuddering, gasping for breath. I felt as if darkness had swallowed me whole, that there were invisible hands stretching forth to strangle me.

The sudden flickering of lamplight threw shadows upon the walls, and without a single moment of delay, I escaped Lord Mathers' room and tore into the hall.

That's when I saw it.

Led by Jared, a procession of servant men carried a large coffin upon their shoulders (I rather think it was the same coffin I hid inside nights before). I was thunderstruck. Lord Mathers was finally dead, and feeling a sudden sense of remorse, I followed the procession out of the castle, across the beautifully manicured garden, and into the bowels of the semi-circular structure. We walked silently down the long, dark, damp passageways until we finally entered a crypt.

"Welcome to the final destination, Mr. Woodward," muttered a familiar voice behind me, a voice that struck a chill into my heart.

I turned around and found Lord Ferdinand Elvin Mathers, very much alive. He stood tall and proud, his eagle's beak of a nose held high in the air, as if he'd never been sick at all.

"I wasn't expecting you," he said. "But since you're here, I wish you to join us in the mourning of my loyal servant, Maverick."

I was stunned. Maverick? But how? I had only just seen him yesterday, and he was perfectly fine.

"I wished to see you and bid you farewell before taking my leave," I said.

The old man gave no response, not even the slightest twitch, though I noticed a very sinister grin on the face of Helena, who was standing in the corner. The entire congregation was dressed in black from head to toe, save for Helena, who wore a red scarf around her neck. She was dreadfully beautiful, as always, but something about her frightened me to death.

Across the crypt stood the mysterious woman of the woods, identical to Helena but with golden hair. What troubled me most were both women's salient features— pale skin, scarlet lips like fresh blood, twinkling eyes like glittering stars in the lurid sky. The resemblance was uncanny, and despite all the angelic beauty bestowed upon them, there tarried a malevolence that seemed to radiate between them.

The burial had still not finished when I noticed Jared the butler standing beside me. My heart began to race; it always had in the past whenever he was around. To me, Jared the butler was a forerunner of misfortune.

"Do you still think of departure?" he asked with a metallic grin.

My lips twitched as I endeavored to respond. "Why shouldn't I? I'm meant to depart this evening."

Jared simply stared at me with a menacing grin. His eyes were as restless as a lone wolf.

"You won't be leaving any time soon, Mr. Woodward," he said. "If at all."

6

Raelyn Atherton's Journal

March 17th, 1903. London

It has been less than a month since Gerard's last letter, but to me it seems like ages. I feel like a dry desert, desperate for water.

My eyes are desperate to see Gerard again. He is my fiancé. My soon-to-be husband. My life. The only thing I hold of utmost value. With his departure, I am forlorn. My closest friend, Jayda, is also out of station, along with her husband to celebrate their first wedding anniversary. I pray that Gerard and I will follow them shortly.

With Jayda out of town and Gerard gone, I feel as if my life is a burden upon my soul. Gracious London is full of mighty people, but unfortunately, none care about a young doctor left without her man, sitting idly by and scratching journals. They might assume I am boring, with no adventures to share, and I don't blame them. I sometimes see myself this same way.

I recall the blessed day when I first met Gerard. I knew from our first glance that he was the man I had always hoped for.

He had come to visit a professional doctor to discuss his acute anxiety—God bless the malady that brought our two souls together. The way he looked into my eyes still brings a thrill of joy to my heart, as if it happened just yesterday. He told me that I was a woman of great beauty and even greater intellect.

I cannot describe how much I appreciate and love him. The days which we have spent together are the sweetest memories I will ever hold, and now I look forward to becoming his wife.

March 25th, 1903

Still no word from Gerard. It's frightening me. God, please protect my man from any and every evil.

I have always loved my profession, but at the present time, it seems a burden upon my shoulders which I cannot bear. My heart churns in the flames of loneliness and despair. Never have I imagined how incomplete Raelyn Atherton could be without Gerard Woodward.

Writing his name soothes not only my heart, but also smooths the flow of my pen.

March 27th, 1903

Received a letter from Jayda today. I'm so glad to hear that she's enjoying quality time with her husband. She plans to stay longer and says she will return to London very soon.

Jayda is more than a friend to me. She is my sister. A beautiful woman who lost her parents when she was just a girl.

Her father was a timber merchant who suddenly disappeared under unknown circumstances. The investigation led to a dead end and no evidence was ever obtained to deduce his fate. Jayda's mother died of an incurable illness, though Jayda believes her father's disappearance also led to her mother's demise. Jayda's account has always left me curious. Was it really her father's unpredictable disappearance, or was it, in some way or another, a larger conspiracy to cover his trail of infidelity? I have always wished to share my opinions with Gerard, but a mingled mortification of absurdity and ignominy holds my tongue. It's a secret, along with one other, which I believe only time shall reveal.

I received yet another letter the following day, hoping it was from Gerard. Despite my disappointment, it brought a little joy to my heart, for my cousin, Nathan Connolly, has written to me from Iceland. He has taken his leave for a month and will be in London next week. I'm so glad that I shall have someone other than my journal to share in my loneliness.

I departed early from work in merriment, visited the church, fed the poor, and did every sort of deed to please my Father in heaven. On my return home, I noticed a miserable man on the cobblestones, with grizzled hair, swollen eyes, and a face which spoke of a thousand sorrows.

I have never seen such a thin man. His whole face seemed sharpened away into nothing but nose and chin, and the skin of his cheeks was drawn tight over his outstanding bones. His tweed suit, pocket watch, and brightly polished stick eliminated my assumption about his poverty, and yet he walked as if he had nothing left in the world except his broken soul. He wasn't old, but his agony made him appear on the brink of his grave.

He proceeded towards the church but ended up climbing the steps to the elevated cemetery beside it, where he sat quietly upon a stone bench. There was a certain innocence in his manner that made me worry about his suffering, and as a result, I slowly approached him.

"I do not converse with strangers," he said sternly, and I was stunned at his rudeness. All the pity I felt for him vanished like a drop of water into sand.

"Doctors have no foul intentions of committing theft in broad daylight," I quipped, and was about to walk away when his harsh voice humbled into a murmur.

"Forgive me," he apologized. "I am neither a wanderer nor a man without manners. I've always been betrayed by the ones I trust, and my poor heart no longer holds the strength to bear it."

"You must be a stronger judge of character, sir. Believe me, everyone is not the same. There are those like me who are devoted to the holy cause and try to help the needy, as preached by Christ."

The old man sighed. There seemed to be a glimmer of relief in his eyes, and the apprehensive furrows of his forehead vanished.

"My name is Mark Huddleston," he said. "I'm a trader from Sussex."

"A trader," I said. "How exciting."

"It's not all it's chalked up to be," he grumbled. "Trade links the globe together, certainly. I have been to different parts of the world and have met people from many different traditions, cultures, and tongues. But while we rejoice over our shared cultures and wear our traditions with pride, so too is evil familiar with every corner of the world. Betrayal follows us all like a shadow we can never escape."

He explained to me that as a student, he had always been interested in history. Collecting artifacts was what he presumed life was all about. He simply loved it.

Once during an eclipse, he was robbed by his own workman, the man whom his entire faith relied upon. But then, something unexpected happened the following day. He found his treacherous workman's dead body floating in the wharf. Based on the state of the body, Huddleston assumed that the workman must have suffered terribly before the grace of death, for his contorted body and fragile back spoke of extreme starvation . . .

As though all the life had been sucked out of him.

"I presumed it to be divine vengeance," Mark Huddleston said with a shrug. "My trade flourished after the death of that man, and I confess that not a single day has passed that I haven't thanked the Almighty for killing him. But good fortune doesn't last forever."

I pressed him further, and Huddleston told me of a Christmas Eve when his ship was attacked by pirates. All his consignment had been robbed, three of his deckhands were slaughtered, and he lost his only means of livelihood. He went on to confess that it had been one of his own men who had worked alongside the pirates to ensure their success.

"The cheap fellow met a terrible accident last year," he said at last, his lips aquiver. "May God bless the owner of that factory, whose heavy machinery crushed that man to death."

Huddleston found further success after the accident, but then described how the woman he loved betrayed him and fled away with her lover.

"Every time I believe my days will get better, they only get worse." He sighed, then clenched his jaw. "One day, she will get what's coming to her."

I saw marks of disdain on his face that, despite speaking of a hundred sorrows, resonated a silent threat. There was a spasm of lunacy upon his face whenever he spoke of divine vengeance, and a measure of pride each time he recalled it.

"Life always finds a way," I said, deciding to take my leave as it was getting late. "You should not despair over your Lord's mercy. He tests us with hardships and trials. What we really need to do is patiently endure, for indeed His help is near."

Mark Huddleston shot a glance at me in the manner of a man whose faith has been provoked, though unintentionally.

"Separations aren't easy either," he snorted. "Your longing for your fiancé isn't as terrible as my afflictions have been."

I felt such a repulsion at his words that, for an instant, I wanted to choke him with my bare hands. Instead, I walked away from Mark Huddleston, scared and amazed.

How does Mark Huddleston know about Gerard?

Lord, please help Gerard reach home safely.

March 30th, 1903

I contemplate my encounter with Mark Huddleston every day I walk to and from church. I've taken the same route and have found no trace of him.

His words regarding Gerard still haunt me. His rude behavior has still not slipped my mind, and I never wish to encounter such a disgraceful person again.

Nathan will be here in a couple of days and the thought excites me more than anything—not as much as Gerard, of course, but I'm in a state of restlessness to meet my cousin after so long. For now, I've got things to do and so I must put down my pen.

It is my heartfelt wish to write about Gerard Woodward's return the next time I return to my journal.

7

Raelyn Atherton's Journal, Continued.

April 3rd, 1903

I am disappointed and embarrassed, for there is still no word from Gerard.

I'm running short of patience. I have a horrible feeling in my heart that something dire has happened. May the Almighty protect me and my loved ones. I swore to myself not to open my journal until I had heard from Gerard, but an abrupt event, like a match struck in darkness, has brought me some hope.

My cousin, Nathan Connolly, arrived in London today. The sight of him was so soothing to my eyes that for a minute or two, I forgot my worries, though they were quick to return. He looked just as I remembered him: a pale, sad-faced, refined-looking man, with black hair and smooth skin.

"It's good to see you, little cousin," he said, rubbing his eyes and staring about in sleepy bewilderment. He patted my shoulder and smiled. "You haven't changed at all."

"Neither have you," I mused, subtly admiring my cousin. "I really wish Gerard was here too. You would have loved his sense of humour."

"Are lawyers humourous?" he asked, winking. "Strange."

"People are not always as they seem," I remarked, and

Nathan couldn't help stifling his laughter. Apparently, I had failed to conceal my possessive nature for Gerard—a trait of mine that Nathan had always poked fun at.

There was something about Nathan, however, that seemed odd. He acted quite peculiar in his manners, for at times, he seemed lost in his thoughts, smiling and muttering under his own breath, and occasionally watching me absentmindedly, as if I was but a dream.

"Is everything all right, Nathan?" I asked, trying to sound casual.

It took a moment or two for him to respond. "I'm fine," he said, stammering. "I am just tired, and I want to rest."

Exhaustion was obvious after such a long journey, and hence I decided not to trouble him anymore. We talked a little whilst our carriage swept across the imperial streets of London. The fog was quite broken up, and a haggard shaft of daylight would occasionally glance in between the swirling wreaths as we advanced towards my mansion. But as soon as our ride stopped and we got out of the carriage, Nathan refused to stay at my house.

"Come now, you can stay a day or two in my home," I said, feeling a little offended. "I'll make sure the estate is properly cleaned before you make for bed."

"I express my sincere gratitude for your concern, cousin, but I don't want to burden you with my responsibilities. The guesthouse will suffice. I'm a grown man and I can take care of myself."

I noticed an unusual glare in his eyes, as if he had said his final word and meant not to argue.

I made a slight bow and we parted ways, me to the mansion and he to the guesthouse.

April 7th, 1903

It hasn't even been a week since Nathan's arrival in London, but his health has declined remarkably. It began to worry me to such an extent that I decided not to leave him alone in my guesthouse, for I suspect he is not maintaining a proper diet.

But again, to my surprise, he rejected my proposal without a moment's consideration. I urged him to see another physician then, in case he doubted my credibility as a doctor, but he very courteously rebuffed.

I might not know what's wrong with my cousin, but something in his disposition has unprecedentedly changed, and my sole intention is to find out why.

April 12th, 1903

Another week has come and gone, and Nathan's health is turning worse.

He has become slender, hollow-cheeked, and red-eyed. He appears much older than his thirty-two years. His hair is grizzly, his eyes feeble, and there is frailty in his gait.

To me, he is an entirely different man, and at times, I doubt if I have ever really known him. He embraces loneliness, something which my cousin, Nathan Connolly, once intensely hated and deeply feared. This stranger (as I have come to think of him) avoids companionship and dislikes my presence whenever I am around him.

There are very occasional moments when he talks to me like I'm his little cousin, and I feel as if I can see a glimpse of the man behind the stranger. But his personality is, most of the time, overwhelmed by a darker side that will not tolerate anyone around him.

Great God, merciful God, please make for Nathan a way out of this desolation.

After giving up on every attempt to establish a successful conversation with my cousin, I left the guesthouse disheartened.

As I was walking back home, I caught a glimpse of the old man, Mark Huddleston, walking towards the chapel. I noticed heavy marks of disquiet hanging over his rigid face, and he turned around quite frequently in order to ensure he wasn't being followed. He cupped his hand against his forehead to shade his eyes from the afternoon sunlight, and I observed his hands shivering constantly, as if he was prone to violent tremors.

I confess that my initial thoughts were ugly and that I presumed he was up to something fishy, but strong waves of regret swirled within my heart when I saw him entering the chapel.

I feel trapped in a world of strangers, where my long-lost Gerard is my only true companion.

April 13th, 1903

I wanted to leave early from the clinic, but unfortunately, the workload was tremendous. I was so delighted, then, to learn that Nathan wanted to see me when I was done.

But what I hoped would be a splendid affair turned absolutely bizarre.

Nathan spoke only nonsense. I am worried that his malady has begun to affect his mind, for what he tried to explain to me is what the psychiatrists term as hallucinations.

I asked to examine him, but he denied. I asked him about these hallucinations, but again, he would not tell me. The least I could do was encourage him to make brief notes on any stress or pain, or any sort of vivid experience that disturbs him.

It seems the only appropriate way to study his mind.

April 15th, 1903

I was awakened by a dreadful nightmare. Never in my entire life have I had such a horrible dream. My heart still trembles at the thought of it.

I was walking on a long, lonely road. A crescent moon glanced occasionally through the misty clouds, giving in form the shadows that lurked here and there along the roadway. A threatening silence lay upon the place.

I suddenly heard the clicking of boot heels against the concrete, the horrifying sound echoing in the dark mists of the deserted street. Whoever was pursuing me I remember not, but my body was drenched in sweat and lacked the strength to flee. I kept trembling and falling as I ran, until at one point, I heard a sharp, hellish wail that devoured my senses. I found myself in such a state of paralysis that I could not even scream.

With a thumping heart and pulsing nerves, I turned around and became struck with such unimaginable horror that I nearly fainted. There before my eyes, and surrounding me from all sides, stood an army of toddlers—if they indeed were toddlers—with pale faces, bloodshot eyes, broad mouths, and every little feature like demons of the pit. I was lying in a pool of blood, restless and numb while sharp, flaming, malicious little eyes flickered from every shadow. I was deathly pale and breathing fast, glancing desperately about my surroundings. One dark and horrible child stepped forward then, held out his hand to me, and I screamed.

I woke up in my bed, breathless and panting, still struggling to regain my calm. To my horror I was, in reality, covered in blood. I nearly collapsed and had to take deep breaths to hold myself upright. I checked for wounds upon my flesh and found none, though my nightgown was steeped in red.

I feel myself consumed in all sorts of terrible imaginations, and only heaven knows what awaits me. The more I think of my nightmare and my bloody nightgown, the more extraordinary and inexplicable it appears.

One thing which I'm resolute and strongly determined for is to visit the church in a couple of hours. Whatever invisible force is lurking behind all this can only be defeated and overcome by the divine power of the Almighty alone.

***

It was such a relief walking into God's gracious door. It felt as if all my fear and worries had suddenly evaporated. I spoke with Father Malcolm about my nightmare, and he advised me to never separate the Lord's crucifix from my body.

"Dreams can sometimes be a warning of impending danger," he said to me, then gave me a vial of holy water and commanded me to sprinkle it around my door and windows. He assured me not to worry, that I should have faith in the Father in heaven.

As an honest Christian woman, I'm a staunch believer in the powers of Christ, and nothing will make me deviate from my religion. My faith is strong and so is God.

My only wish is for Gerard to return.

April 16th, 1903

My nightmare was nothing compared to what I witnessed today.

Nathan's health has turned pathetic, as though his very own soul struggles to remain intact within his body. His lifestyle has become extremely unhygienic, and I honestly doubt whether this particular individual, in the slightest reality, is Nathan Connolly.

I was hesitant to speak with him, but his fluctuating behaviour surprised me again. He sounded polite today, also guilty, and was willing to take any piece of advice from, as he called me, Dr. Raelyn Atherton. I prescribed for him a healthy diet, along with proper rest, to which he very gallantly accepted.

I also offered him some holy water, which he quite nastily discarded.

I need to see Father Malcolm at the earliest.

8

Nathan Connolly's Notes

April 19th, 1903

I feel so relieved whenever my doctor, who also happens to be my cousin, Raelyn Atherton, visits me. She is beautiful and her voice is melodious, which brings comfort not only to my ears, but also soothes my grieving heart.

How fortunate is the lawyer who will soon be taking her as his wife. But Gerard's ongoing absence saddens me. The fact that he neglects her advice and does not write sets her heart ablaze and, at times, triggers the rage within me. No one—not even her fiancé—has the right to hurt Raelyn. I worry for her just like she worries for me. I am aware that my condition troubles her. How else can a person witness her cousin slipping further into the grip of death each day?

My emotions are endless, but I shall limit my notes with things I was told to mention. Raelyn wants me to pen down every stress, pain, and hallucination I experience.

The first point I will mention is absolute fear. I feel distressed over my declining condition, and it comes with such terror. I feel myself trapped in a situation which, to me, seems endless and bound with delusions. I sense menacing shadows sneaking in the dark, and a pair of sinister eyes that are always fixed upon me. It so happened one night when Raelyn had left my house after examining my health.

I take pride in writing that I am a man of strong faith and solitary ambition. I've never developed ill feelings for any person, and the respect I have for my cousin is beyond measure. But things were about to turn ugly, and the night of April 12th was the milestone.

Raelyn's presence has always comforted me, but on that particular night, I feared when she came calling to the guesthouse. There was a gleam in her savoury eyes, like that of a ferocious cat that might, at any moment, devour her prey.

"Do you fear death?" she asked with a grin, and I was thunderstruck. I was aware of my nearing fate, but her atrocious audacity was something I had never witnessed before. I knew Raelyn would never speak of my demise anywhere around me, especially in my current condition. In fact, she scolded me like a child each time I mentioned my own approaching end.

The woman before me looked like Raelyn, but those were not her words—I know this deep within myself. I give my solemn word upon it.

"I know you have been troubled by my malady," I replied. "I sincerely apologize for it. I hope you are relieved from my burden as quickly as possible, and I pray that you are reunited with Gerard Woodward very soon. May you live and love as you deserve. My only wish is to be able to kiss your child, should you ever have one, before I return to the black earth."

She sighed, more annoyed than saddened.

"Do not speak of Gerard," she barked. "He does not love me anymore. He is a selfish bastard. I no longer look upon him as the man of my dreams. To be honest, I do not even look upon him as a man at all. May he eternally reside in hell!"

"What is the matter with you, cousin?" I roared, almost immediately upon her conclusion. I expected an answer, but to my amazement, she rose furiously, stared at me in utmost hatred, and fled away out the door and into the night.

I may sound delusional, but I still swear that this woman wasn't Raelyn Atherton.

I was chained in desolation, and yet this misery became unbearable when I crossed paths with another disaster. I confess, ashamedly so, to having had a nocturnal emission on that resentful night and I felt myself weakened like never before.

But the biggest blow happened the following morning when I met with Raelyn. One could hardly imagine my state of mind upon learning that it wasn't my beloved cousin who visited me last night, for she told me she had been at the clinic, consumed in paperwork, and thus had never come to the guesthouse. What made me believe her words was the gentleness in her manner, the slightest shade of which had been missing from the disposition of the woman I encountered last night.

"You must have been dreaming, my dear Nathan," she said in her pleasant voice, filled with both compassion and care. "You stress over your condition, cousin. You must stay hopeful and strong and pray to God that everything shall pass."

I relate this incident with a heavy heart and a sorrowful mind. But this was only the beginning. My fear has already taken over a large part of me. I have begun to dream every time that I sleep, and always wake up wet and exhausted. It has become a new routine, and what troubles me most is the repeating of the same dream, again and again. It is always the same.

The only thing I know is that the mystery behind my malady may just lie behind these dreams of mine.

April 23rd, 1903

I try constantly to be rid of my dreams and strive hard to seek answers, but I constantly fail. Not only has my fruitlessness shattered my heart, but it has extinguished even the slightest hope within me that things will soon get better.

I shall now disclose the vision that has been recently disturbing me in the gloom:

Each night I slip into the dark, I dream of a captivating maiden walking towards me in a sheer fabric of silk. Her bare thighs, her waist, and her deep, smooth cleavage appear like shining pearls found deep beneath the surface of the sea. Her eyes are so magnetic that they draw the two poles of the earth together as one. Her fragrance is more superior than jasmine. I fail to summon words that could ever describe the sensitivity of her delicate lips, perfect hues that outshine the petals of rose. It brings a thrill to my entire body, despite being but a dream.

But what follows next is equally agonizing and doleful, for I find myself lying in a pool of blood. I no longer feel or see the beautiful maiden, but a heavy weight upon me keeps me nailed to the ground like a sheep in a slaughterhouse. I try with all my heart, vigour, and soul to perceive the thing atop me, but I find my vision blurred. I feel a strong choke around my neck, and then I wake up perspiring and in shortness of breath, only to discover myself stuck with nocturnal emission.

I may never know, but I strongly feel that my dreams

are in some way the reason for my decay. I do not have the heart to speak about it to my cousin. I believe my notes will do what my tongue cannot. Raelyn shall eventually find them one day when I'm gone, and then she will be relieved of bearing this unnecessary burden of mine.

April 25th, 1903

I did something strange this day that the normal me could never dare to think about. But I feel delighted to remember it was Maria's request for me to do so. How else can a man build a strong bond with the woman he loves, unless he is willing to fulfill her every desire?

I agree that many might call it horrible. I myself was stunned to hear that my precious Maria wished me to eat a live rat.

She says that she wants me to be strong, and I must confess that I trust her now more than I trust Raelyn. There is still a fog of dubiousness encircling my mind, as to whether my encounters with this princess are real, or a mere dream; but regardless, I love Maria more than any other thing on this earth, perhaps more than the Almighty himself.

Maria says she will never leave me, and I believe her.

It has been difficult to look into my cousin's eyes ever since my new love assigned me this secret task. I know Raelyn suspects something strange ever since I forced her to purchase a rat trap.

She worries about me. I like it, though now she visits me more frequently. This I despise. I wish I could tell her that I don't need her anymore. I have Maria and she is enough for a man like me. I don't care if the whole world turns upside down—all I need is Maria, and that will suffice.

I have been a little harsh with Raelyn lately, but it is for her own good. Perhaps she will realize I don't need her and will leave me alone. Nothing else matters to me now, for I have found the peace that I have been longing for. Let it be known to all!

It is getting dark, and my heart is racing with anticipation. The time to meet with my Maria is approaching, and damn every other thing that gets in the way.

9

Nathan Connolly's Notes, Continued

April 29th, 1903

Had a heated argument with Raelyn. I think my words have wounded her deeply, and I also acted in a way which I presently regret. But I don't bother much about her thoughts. As long as I have Maria by my side, Raelyn can burn in hell. What shocks me more is how violent, and at times, vulnerable, an innocent woman like Raelyn can be. She thinks she is superior to me. She pretends she cares for me and can look after me. I don't need her affections. In fact, I don't need her at all. She can save her condolences for Gerard Woodward.

But I don't want to waste my memories, or the ink, writing about Raelyn.

This brings me to my beloved Maria. I love her and, as such, I have kept my word. She has requested I feed on rats all these days and nights, and my stomach hasn't gone a single day without its flesh. The rats smell and are hard to palate, but I shall continue consuming them for her.

She says my health is improving and I look much better than before. I believe her. She has destroyed all the mirrors in the guesthouse where I stay, but I can see myself through her eyes. I trust her honesty. Her affection and care for me is real, unlike Raelyn, who thinks I am insane.

Sick. A feeble lunatic driven to fantasy and delusion.

I don't give a damn.

The rage I feel for my cousin reminds me of an incident that happened last night, which although beautiful in the beginning turned ugly at last. I curse Raelyn for not leaving my mind at ease. But then, I love Maria and so I found respite in the way it ended.

I was dead asleep, covered with my blanket from head to toe and succumbed to darkness. I felt a sudden weight crawling on top of me. My body, despite its delirium, was filled with a heavenly thrill, and my heart pounded with delight.

Maria was all that my mind could imagine, mounting me to present me with her heavenly pleasures. My longing for togetherness and my acute impatience brought me out of my slumber. As I removed the blanket from my face, I found myself paralyzed, too helpless and horrified to move. My fearful eyes gaped up at a large, furious cat of pitch black stretched over my chest. Her whiskers appeared like that of a hungry lion, while her eyes were charged with utmost malice.

The scene left me petrified, but an abrupt surge in my adrenaline and the grotesque hunger that followed shook me to the core. So carried was I in the flame of revenge, that it took a very long time for me to realize that the cat had suddenly died. I simply could not bear the truth that the evil of this animal had dared to interrupt my beautiful moments with Maria.

I fail to recall much.

All I can remember is the taste of its blood dripping from my mouth.

May 1st, 1903

I love walking in the deserted streets under the dim moonlight, especially when Maria requests me to do so. I have been doing it ever since our first encounter. In walking these moonlit streets, I have been witness to things one can hardly dream of.

Maria conceals nothing from me, and this makes my love for her grow ever stronger. I have been living with lies up to this moment, yet now I live in truth.

I cannot mention any of our plans though, lest Raelyn's cunning eyes should discover them someday and our cause would be lost. I shall never let that happen. Now I'm entirely capable of distinguishing between friends and foes. I have also successfully overcome my weaknesses.

Maria says I am fit to carry out the chore ...

All she has to do is say it.

10

Letter from Ralph Brewer
to Father Malcolm Isaac Simpson

February 24, 1903
Swindon

Reverend Father,

I might not be a familiar name, but let it be known that I am a close companion to both Gerard Woodward and Raelyn Atherton.

I'm writing to you regarding the woman I love, though she doesn't love me. She never has. Her heart belongs to only one man—Mr. Woodward, the famed and fortunate European advocate and lawyer, who despite his lady's repeated pleas, has decided to visit a remote castle in Cardiff. To my knowledge, this castle belongs to Lord Ferdinand Elvin Mathers, the only surviving grandchild of Lord Marlowe Elvin Mathers the Great, who played quite a significant role in the war against Napoleon, during which his planned invasion of Great Britain was uprooted.

Lord Marlowe, along with a small community of Jews, acted as a barrier to safeguard the Mathers' family land from the French. Matherses have always been a proud race, though I've heard whispers among some renowned scholars relating to certain events that could tarnish their reputation. What this confidential study is all about I know not, for I am not at all interested in history.

This brings me to the point:

Raelyn feels something abhorrent in her fiancé's whole expedition. She says there is a veiled danger that cannot be ignored, a danger that troubles her like hell. She needs your help, Father. I am an agnostic creature, with absolutely no room for religion or hope. But Raelyn is a true follower of Christ, exactly the kind of person you and your organization entertain, or to be more specific, are willing to stretch your helping hands for. She needs it.

She wrote to me even before Gerard's departure. It's a secret, but I believe that it won't be so for long, for the lady in love discloses everything to her fiancé. I hardly care.

You are a holy priest who holds an important and sacred position in our society. I admit that I was a bit baffled at the sight of you—Malcolm the priest, a large man with rounded shoulders, a massive head, and a broad, intelligent face, sloping down to a pointed beard of grizzled brown. To me, you appeared more like the captain of a ship.

Forgive me if I have offended you, for by now, you must be aware that religion doesn't suit me in the slightest. I do not believe what my eyes do not perceive. Both Gerard and Raelyn have always thought ill of me for this. Raelyn herself would have written to you, I am sure, had your transfer not taken place, a transfer that carried you away from your homeland.

Gerard Woodward is an ambitious man, Father. He will not turn down the offer of Lord Mathers, no matter how much his future bride beseeches. There are horrible tales of northern Cardiff; I believe this is what scares Raelyn. Stories that are told to frighten young children to sleep. Raelyn is evidently desperate for Gerard's return, even before his departure, which makes me jealously admire her pure love for my friend.

She needs your help, Father. I would be eternally grateful to you if you would aid her cause.

What truly worries me is the catastrophe taking place in our town, for the case of missing children has been reported for a sixth consecutive time. Infants are disappearing each night, and the plagues of fear and loathing are spreading like wildfire within every heart. Everyone in town is afraid. I am afraid there is a lunatic running loose in the streets, and unfortunately, I'm the sole believer of this theory. Others proclaim it to be a demonic force. But whatever the cause, it needs to be sorted out.

Who knows whether both events are somehow related, but I hope you of all men can solve this great and terrible mystery.

Your propitious aid is requested here in the east of the island, and in London, where Raelyn Atherton would indeed be indebted to you, as always.

My regards.

Yours sincerely,

Ralph Brewer

11

Raelyn Atherton's Journal

May 3rd, 1903

A bitter sob cuts through my throat whilst I sit down this day to write. My heart is severely wounded by none other than my cousin, Nathan Connolly.

He hates me. This is evident.

Cousins who have never once argued in their entire lives have recently begun to despise each other. We get into heated arguments quite often these days. What was ugliest in this whole set of affairs, however, was the fact that Nathan wanted to hit me. He raised his hand to slap me, and he would have succeeded had it not been for the surprise arrival of my best friend, Jayda. She walked in seeking my counsel and saved me from his wrath right in time.

Nathan has drastically changed. I feel it in my bones. It gives me a chill to write this down, but I fear he is involved in something dreadful and inhumane. I remember how oddly savage and obstinate he was while asking me to buy a rat trap. I might, at times, have considered it a joke and would have also laughed at it, but the awful memory has attached itself to the inside of my skull. Nathan almost lost his temper when I refused, threatened me with dire consequences, and did not relent until I had to finally submit to his stubbornness.

I might have sat and mourned for an entire lifetime if my best friend, Jayda, hadn't returned, which I took as a good sign of fortune. She has remarkably changed ever since her return from Bristol. Her beauty has intensified, say it for her rosy cheeks, her slender neck, the perfect curls of her hair, and her long eyelashes that flutter like the wings of a butterfly. Her high cheekbones, delicate chin, and lips of pinkish hue give her a regal appearance like those splendid beauties who are fashioned to remain in palaces and castles in tales of the old. Jayda is mesmerizing in both her mien and speech. I sometimes ponder how blessed and fortunate her husband is. She loves Justin, perhaps more than he loves her.

Jayda's arrival has blared courage into my heart.

"What is wrong with your cousin?" she asked me as we stepped out of the guesthouse. "I've never seen him behave in such a manner."

"Neither have I," I answered with a pained heart. "I'm scared he isn't Nathan Connolly anymore. He's a completely different creature, a stranger I don't even know."

"What makes you say these things, my dear?"

I gulped, the blood frozen in my veins. And when I spoke, I let go of everything I had been holding in my heart.

"I agree that I have been working a lot. My heart is grieving and longing for Gerard, but I assure you that my eyes weren't deceived by what they saw, nor was I caught up in hysteria. During my recent visits to Nathan, I smelled something sinister in the situation, something horrible, for whenever I entered the guesthouse I could sense the metallic smell of blood, and a very foul stench of rotten flesh. Nathan's terrible hygiene and filthy surroundings are far worse than any London slum. I asked him about it, and then he sharply rejected my suggestions and commanded me not to interfere in his life. He said he would be fine and that I should worry about myself. I was hurt, to be frank. I felt as if I was no longer needed and so, I walked straight out of that hell.

"It was two nights later when I returned to the guesthouse to apologize. I wanted to settle things between us. As I was walking towards the guesthouse, I sensed a figure moving in the shadows. I was being followed, I'm sure of it. I hurried down the path, careful enough to turn around in order to catch a glimpse of my pursuer, but I saw nothing. Then suddenly, in the silence, I heard a sound that sent my heart into my mouth. It was as quick as lightning, but it was real, I'm certain of it. I heard steps on the cobblestone path, echoing in the night until it died away. At one point, I felt as if someone was right behind me, but when I looked back, I found myself the only person on the deserted road. It was all so real that it still raises the hair on my arms just to think of it."

Jayda listened to me with utmost attention, so I continued.

"When I stepped inside the guesthouse, it was yet another disaster, much greater and more terrifying than what I had just endured on the path. I cannot imagine a more horrid picture. I was about to dash away in a state of extreme fright, but Nathan's voice suddenly stopped me.

"There were patches of dried blood staining his bed and along the walls and furniture. He must have been cautious enough to cleanse his gaunt face, but I observed that from the corner of his lips protruded the dark tail of a rat, which he hastily and very casually pushed into his mouth as if it were the most normal thing in the world.

He stared at me with a pair of cunning eyes and a face like that of a fiend. I was disturbed and horror-stricken to such an extent that I hurriedly and hesitantly asked about his health, and then took my leave without a moment's delay.

"But as I was walking out of his room, I noticed an antique vase that surely wasn't mine. It looked like some ancient piece of pottery with some sacred scripture carved on its outer surface. The jar was so unique that I'm sure you wouldn't find anything similar if you visited every museum in the world. As I left Nathan alone in the guesthouse, something struck my mind. I grew cold thinking about it."

"What?" enquired Jayda impatiently. "What worried you?"

"The artifact!" I cried. I opened my mouth to speak more of the odd vase, but strangely, no words came from my mouth, no matter how hard I tried.

Jayda's face was grave. She did not respond for a very long time, perhaps to deduce her own assumptions.

Then, taking a deep breath, she answered, "I see that you have been exposed to this misery for quite some time now, my friend. This illness seems to be spreading from Nathan's body and into his mind, but what can one do against the will of God? You have done your best. I suggest that you stay away from your cousin for a while. Who knows, it might help him recover. Miracles do happen, after all. I sincerely apologize for my late return home, but now that I am back, I will remain beside you regardless of the situation."

Her words were a comfort to my crippled heart. Jayda is a sister to me, and with her presence, I know I can withstand any hardship.

May 4th, 1903

Bright mornings in London have always refreshed my soul; but things seemed different when I woke up this morning. I had a task at hand, and with Jayda's support, I was willing to take new risks that also involved crossing mountains, if need be.

I took my leave from work and made my way straight to church. I waited a long time in the cemetery for Mark Huddleston, but the old man never showed up. With a repellent sentiment of defeat, I started home.

I had the urge to pay Nathan a visit, for his recent activities have deeply saddened me, and I daresay that he has turned into an entirely different man. Such a great and unexpected change points to madness, but in view of Nathan's manner and words, there must be some deeper meaning. I regret my failure, for I have failed to secure my cousin and bring him back to normalcy. He hates me so intensely that he no longer has the patience to endure my presence.

I lacked the courage to stop by the guesthouse, for it is not only Nathan but also his abode that has begun to frighten me. Whilst I was trailing across the street, I heard a group of teenagers gossiping. What intimidated them vehemently I know not, but there were heavy marks of trepidation upon their faces, and eyes that stared in evident horror.

"Did you hear what happened last night?" asked the taller one amongst them. To me, he seemed to be a lad of around nineteen years of age, gray eyes fixed keenly upon his mates. Apparently, a dog belonging to a man named Mr. Hawkins was mauled in his home. The family was out for dinner, save for the housemaid who retired to her own chamber and came running when a terrible wail fell onto her ears. She says it didn't take her long to arrive in the foyer, and whatever savage creature was behind the attack had already vanished, save for a pool of blood and small bits of flesh scattered all over the floor.

As I walked by, I noticed their pale faces, and my heart felt feeble. I know of a similar incident which still agonizes my heart, where the subject of that particular tragedy was a rat.

I can only pray to the good Lord that the events aren't interrelated.

12

Letter from Father Malcolm Isaac Simpson to Raelyn Atherton

May 5, 1903
Swindon

Dear Miss Atherton,

My sincere apologies for such an unusual delay in writing back to you. I know you have been anxious ever since Gerard neglected your advice and took his departure for Cardiff. I can only imagine how a lady like you must feel upon hearing no word from her fiancé after such a long time.

I applaud your decision to write to Ralph Brewer on the very day before Gerard's departure, for you might never know what vital part it had played in saving a life. I can't fathom the outcome that might have occurred had you chosen not to act. Again, I appreciate your courage, your sincerity, and your unshakable love that could move mountains and forge irons.

I once again apologize for writing to you so late, for I have been waylaid by circumstances that I never could have dreamed of.

Ralph Brewer wrote to me in your name, explaining

to me your dire situation ever since Gerard accepted the invitation to Lord Mathers' castle.

Speaking plainly, Miss Atherton, you must leave for Swindon at once. There is no time to inquire further about your visit; rather, begin your journey forthwith. We've got a lot to talk about once you arrive.

Make absolutely sure that no one knows about my letter, or of your departure. I mean no exceptions.

Forever in service to humanity.

Yours faithfully,

Father Malcolm Simpson

13

Jayda Pearson's Diary

May 6th, 1903

I am overwrought, and it soothes me to express myself here. I feel inclined to continue writing and never stop, for I have a sea of emotions to note.

What bothers me most is the sudden departure of my dear friend, Raelyn, who without giving a word has abandoned me. I have no idea why she has left or where she has gone, but what is most heartbreaking is that she never spoke to me about it—me, whom she perpetually claims to be her sister in bond, if not in blood; nor did she bid me farewell before departing.

I expect answers once she returns.

I'm much too confused to reach any certain conclusion at this point. The suspense is becoming dreadful.

I remember Raelyn speaking of an old man, a man named Mark Huddleston, sitting at the cemetery and grieving over his past. What reminded me so suddenly about him is the man himself, for whilst Justin and I had gone to visit the church this morning, I saw him sitting idly by and gazing at the hollow.

Wondering if he knew where my friend had gone, I approached him.

I appreciate the quality with which my friend Raelyn had described him, for upon looking at him, I saw exactly the same disposition. Brilliantly descriptive Raelyn. I remember Raelyn had called him odd, loud, and also rude. To me, however, he seemed to be a gentle soul embracing all the sweetness of this material world before death might, at any moment, carry him away. He certainly was a talker, a man who could go on gossiping until the sun submits to the gloom. Initially, he seemed eager to discover my name, but it was only Justin who participated in the conversation. I think my husband indeed liked this old man; every now and then, I saw him smiling and staring at the old man with marked bewilderment.

I once made an attempt to inquire about his first encounter with Raelyn, to which he, quite peculiarly, inclined his head to indicate that he had indeed met her. It seemed as if they simply made casual introductions, and that there was nothing serious ever discussed between them. This piqued my curiosity.

I tried to ask Mr. Huddleston about his profession, but he very quickly switched the topic, paying more attention to my husband. At last, after their long conversation was over, Mr. Huddleston rose to his feet around dusk, hobbled down the stairs, and disappeared down one of the lanes.

I watched him go, then turned my face to the church. I suddenly felt sick, my mind flooding with a thousand venomous doubts and suspicions.

May 7th, 1903

This morning was bright, and I took it as a perfect opportunity to look for Mark Huddleston. I thought the man might open his heart if I met with him alone. Perhaps it had been the presence of my husband that made him more reserved toward me during our last encounter. I was rigid in mind and in manner to talk to the old man, and he to me.

Though I remained steadfast in my search for him, my hope crumbled to dust once I reached the church. The old man was nowhere to be found. I waited in the cemetery, on the very same stone bench where I last remember him seated.

But Mark Huddleston never showed up.

I sat in silence and rejoiced over the echo of the hymns coming from the church. It was such a great pleasure to my heart that I felt my energy lift.

While I gazed across the street, I caught a glimpse of a dull and shadowy figure emerging from one of the lanes. At first, I thought it to be Mark Huddleston, but both to my astonishment and contempt, it was a strange man dressed in the manner of a gentleman, a manner that least suited him.

He seemed austere with himself, this man, or perhaps pretended to be. He wore a shiny hat and, strangely, a handkerchief tied around his face. All I could see of him were a pair of eyes that watched me with intent before he finally slipped away into an alley.

I daresay villainous people do exist.

The hot glare of late afternoon finally softened into a mellow glow. After spending a while in the chapel, which was unintentional and a way to rid myself of the worry that came upon me at the sight of the strange man across the lane, I started back for home.

I felt enlightened and empowered, for as a staunch believer in Christ my King, I prayed in the chapel and gave my word of honour that evil, however great, can only be defeated by God's mercy, for the Almighty is all powerful and all wise. There's no denying it.

As I walked, I trailed across a group of women, all blushing and giggling amid their private conversation. They were clad in fancy corsets, skirts, and veils drawn over their hats. I wondered after their brooding fashion.

I walked past Raelyn's estate and the guesthouse where Nathan Connolly sleeps, and a sudden movement behind the blinds caught my attention. Through the gap I saw Nathan Connolly himself, before he immediately disappeared from my sight and hid himself behind the wall.

He had been watching me, and I saw, almost in an instant, a dark shadow pass over his face.

I must confess that Raelyn's cousin has begun to frighten me.

Justin and I decided to go out for dinner. I have always loved it. Each moment spent with my husband is better than heaven itself. It makes me realize how much I love him. Walking hand-in-hand with my love is what my heart truly desires.

We suddenly happened upon a small group of people who had gathered before a two-storey building that had no windows, just a door on the lower storey and a blind forehead of discoloured wall on the upper. We stopped the cart and got out.

A man stood at the front, whom I presumed to be a detective, carefully taking notes of whatever the people had to say. The faces I saw were haggard and thin and eager, stamped with the print of a recent horror. Upon getting closer, I felt my heart stop, for the small garden that served as a partition between the doorstep and the boundary was bathed in red.

Blood spilled over the walls and across the grass, while the remains of some poor domestic animal had been strewn about the ground. I would have collapsed to the ground had my husband not held me up.

A queer thought came to my mind as I glanced at a petrified woman weeping on her husband's arm. She was a placid-faced woman, with large, gentle eyes, and grizzled hair curving down over her temples on each side. It struck a chilling cold into my heart, for I recognized her as one of the veiled ladies I had seen earlier, one who gossiped and tittered about with her intimates.

It finally made sense who Nathan Connolly had been staring at from his window, and why he had concealed himself.

I'm glad that I have Justin by my side, for I know he is my protector and my strongest companion. Only my husband could calm me down after such a horrible scene.

Despite the catastrophe, we still went to dinner, and upon our return I caught a glimpse of Nathan's house through the window of our cart. It was still, and it appeared to me as if no one was home inside the stone villa. It made me wonder whether or not my theory was pertinent, or a mere assumption that might slander the poor, wretched man should I speak my assumptions.

Afterwards, I lay stretched on my bed, relaxed yet pondering the recent chain of events that had shaken both Raelyn and now me. My body was at ease as a result of the exquisite, sensational lovemaking with my husband, the fragrance of which my body carried with pride. But my mind was rebellious. I couldn't help thinking about the bloody and harrowing incident we'd seen earlier, a visage that I was afraid would leave a lasting mark upon my mind.

It was right at that moment when my ears perked up at a sudden noise outside our bedroom door. At first, I thought myself to be delusional, too soaked up in my own imagination to differentiate between fantasy and reality. But my husband also arose from his slumber, and this was what filled my heart with dread.

"Did you hear it too?" asked Justin, his eyes knitted in suspicion.

With a mingled hesitance, both Justin and I got out of bed and sidled towards the door. To me, it sounded as if someone was trailing barefoot across our passage, and I wondered if it was a burglar. When we opened the door, there was no one. We heard the click of our front door closing shut, and as Justin threw it open, a sudden repugnance made me weak in every limb.

My eyes witnessed a bloody track starting from our doorstep and running down the long street, until it finally vanished across the narrow lane. All manners of fearful and vivid imaginations filled my mind whilst I cautiously and very steadily followed the track beside my husband. I whimpered and trembled all the way, holding tight to his arm as my personal shield against the looming danger. The night was chilly and dark. There was no sign of life as far as my eyes could see, rather a silent threat in the night's bearing which spoke of a thousand devilish possibilities.

The bloody track was eventually lost. My head buzzed, and I could hardly stand firm beside my husband.

Suddenly, a chill came upon me. I wondered if, quite possibly, it had been a trap set to lure us out of our nest.

I looked up at my husband, who hesitated, and then,

as if upon some sudden reflection, fronted about with an air of defiance. There was a flicker of exasperation over his face, and I knew he would show no mercy if ever it proved to be some sort of mischief; this I honestly doubt, for the recent happenings have given rise to theories of a beast lurking in the shadows. Earlier, the police thoroughly searched the area, but no evidence of a beast was found.

The lane we stood upon ran perpendicular to the broad roadway, where again we saw nothing and no one whilst we walked. Then, to my shock, we abruptly stopped. Under the bridge and down a rugged path sat a dark and dreadful abyss in the gloom. Here, we heard the distinct sound of footsteps, mingled with another that sounded dreadfully like flesh being ripped from bone.

As we listened, there was a sudden break in the rhythm, followed by a suppressed groan, as if whoever was making the noise had become distracted by the tapping of our steps.

What sat down there I know not, but its presence had an appalling, abhorrent, and quite an alarming effect upon my mind. The mewl shrunk into a diabolical sigh and became lost deep into the mist. A momentary stillness followed—a hideous, awful silence that made my stomach churn.

Then, our eyes were exposed to such a ghastly, hellish view that even now, around dawn and seated in my bedroom, I shiver pathetically as if struck with some plague.

A pair of glowing, malicious, yellow eyes glared from the gloom. But before the fiend with the ivory eyes could step into the light, a pebble flew through the air from behind us, reverberating a rough clang as it hit the steel bridge.

The eyes dissolved into the dark mist, and as we turned around, there wasn't a soul to be seen. Justin and I ran across the street in a state of desperation but saw no man or woman.

The entire event happened within a blink of an eye, and when my senses stabilized, I found myself stuck in a web of mysteries.

14

Raelyn Atherton's Journal

May 8th, 1903. Swindon

Gerard! Good heavens!

You answered my prayers, oh God. My fiancé is here. Endless praises and glory be to you, Lord, for you not only saved my man but also reunited him with me after such a long separation. My heart melted into an ocean of sorrow when I saw him lying unconscious on a bed in the monastery.

Gerard appears very weak. His face has grown feeble and pale to his very lips, and there has come a blackness about his eyes. Though he's not as baleful as my cousin Nathan, my fiancé's health has rapidly deteriorated. How I worry so! I've been quite a close observer of Nathan, and I pray to the good Lord that none of Nathan's shadow befalls Gerard.

It was so relieving, so wonderful to be able to finally kiss him. I wanted to wake him up, embrace him, quarrel with him, kiss him even more deeply, hold him tightly in my arms, and never let go of him again. I wanted to speak with him and learn about his experience at Mathers Castle, for surely whatever tragedy might have befallen him must have had its root spread deep within the soil of Cardiff.

But Father Malcolm insisted I let him sleep, for

Gerard required plenty of rest for a speedy recovery. His gracious words were such a relief to my agonizing heart that it intensified my audacity—my determination to do anything in my control, and also beyond, as far as the love of my life was concerned.

Gerard is resting. He now looks peaceful, though still fragile, but I'm here to take care of his every need. Looking at him is such a comfort to my eyes. I feel so alleviated whilst I write, holding his hand.

God is great.

Had a notable conversation with Father Malcolm. He's a man of excellence and brilliance, yet he is as humble as any man can be, affectionate, soothing, and fully dedicated to the Church. To me, he is an inspiration, a guide, and a true preacher of Christ.

"You did wonderfully, Miss Atherton!" he said, settling on the other side of the table. "You have proved how strong a woman can be. Your faith is strong and your mind definite. You are the reason why Gerard is alive."

"Gerard was strong too, wasn't he, Father?" I responded. "He did not relent despite the consequences. His courage and determination has kept him alive in whatever trap he was enclosed in."

Father Malcolm smiled. I noticed the bright yellow in his eyes, a reflection of the fireplace behind me.

I was hesitant to ask, but also enslaved by my own curiosity.

"What's wrong with Gerard, Father?" I finally asked. "Was it the old man's sickness? Something foreign in that damned castle? Or is there an entirely different story behind his condition?"

Father Malcolm was in evident stress but the resolution in his wise face never passed away. "Miss Atherton, I assure you that he will be fine. If it is the details of his journey that bother you, then I'm afraid I don't have much to share."

"You know something, Father, don't you?" I asked with a flicker of impatience. "Please do not conceal even the slightest of truths from me. I beg you. Tell me all that Gerard has experienced and I swear to make myself of any use to you and your heavenly service."

He sighed. "Your love is strong. I never doubt it, for its existence was the sole factor that brought Gerard back to you. Regarding his stay in the castle, I take some respite in telling you that behind those cold, stone walls, Gerard was constantly writing. He was wise enough to record every single detail in his journal. It is a great account for me to study and to fancy a way out of this desolation where we are presently trapped."

"His journal?" I repeated with a flush of surprise, as I suddenly remembered it. "How could I not think about it? Gerard is a habitual writer. His journal? Can I look at it, Father?"

"You cannot," he plainly refused.

"Why not?" I asked, offended.

"Because it is too early," he said. "I cannot endanger any innocent life until I myself have thoroughly examined the contents of the journal and the perils Gerard has suffered. It is a most extraordinary case, and equally frightening."

"I cannot sit idly by and do nothing."

"Evil obeys no rules, Miss Atherton. It does not always act for a reason."

His words had such an adverse effect upon me that for a moment, I was overwhelmed with dizziness. Then came an abrupt surge in my adrenaline, but before I could express my discontent, Father Malcolm interfered.

"I understand how you must be feeling, Miss Atherton," he pacified. "Trust me, I understand how much it must hurt you to watch your fiancé in such a state. What must be equally painful for you is the case with your cousin. I know everything. You need to be patient, my child. We stand at a critical point where toiling with these events may come at a terrible price. I'm advancing into the case of Mr. Woodward, but you need to make a start before you act."

I was startled, for I could not comprehend in the slightest what he meant about me making a start. I was flummoxed and speechless and had no idea about my next move—until dusk approached.

***

After leaving Gerard as well as he could be in his state, I was assigned a room in the monastery, which to my pleasure, was located on the first floor. The room was well furnished and brightly lit, with squared windows that opened to a beautiful lawn, bordered with shrubs of every kind. The walls were richly plastered, the ceilings partially vaulted, often with arched intersections and painted bands emphasizing the architectural design, with pictures filling the remainder of space.

Father Malcolm, to me, seemed quite odd in one thing. He never spoke a word despite my repeated pleas to see Gerard's journal. Instead, he instructed me to meet with a woman who would be paying me a visit shortly.

"You'll know what to do once you meet her," he said imperatively. "Remember, you need to make a start. One cannot get to one's destination unless one moves." These were his only words before he led the young woman inside my chamber, and then he left.

At first, I deduced that the woman needed immediate medical attention. Norah, for that was her name, was rather above the middle height, slim, with dark hair and eyes, which seemed darker against the somewhat transparent pallor of her skin. She was Dutch; at least, so her accent denoted. I don't think that I have ever seen such deathly paleness in a woman's face. Her lips, too, were bloodless, though her eyes were alive with angst.

"You must be quite close to the holy Father Malcolm," she rattled in a broken tone that came out with many gasps and babbles. "You must be, or else he would never let you hear what I have to say."

"What is it that troubles you so much?" I asked anxiously. The woman said not a word, but instead glared at me with repulsive eyes. Finally, after a few moments, she spoke.

"Do you still not understand what your man has gone through?" she asked with utmost scorn. "You're fortunate beyond measure to be able to reunite with your fiancé, for not all share the same fate. Evil has its own strength. I never believed it, not until I saw it with my own eyes. Secrecy is the door of devilry, my dear, and crossing that door comes at a dreadful price, for we mere mortals are highly vulnerable against the dark forces of nature."

She was restless and uneasy, and I noticed her sweaty hands convulsively clasping and unclasping.

"What did you see?" I asked calmly.

"Children," replied Norah, her eyes wide-stretched in horror.

"Children?"

"You might think that I'm out of my senses, but this is the truth. Mothers of my town complain that their children, who appear normal during the day, change characteristics in the dark—bright skin, remarkable strength, yellow eyes, and voices quite different from those of normal infants and toddlers. They appear dreadfully beautiful, and their skin as radiant as the moon. But they possess a false bearing in their manners, and their eyes can swoon an innocent mother with a simple glance. Womenfolk complain that their babies are being, well, replaced during the night by something."

Her words came out with such earnestness that I found it hard to question her. Norah talked to me continuously, narrating the chain of events that she had either witnessed or heard, and, astoundingly, it reminded me of something which I dare not confess to my own soul.

Father Malcolm wants me to visit Norah's town. He says he will accompany me on my errand, and that Gerard will be given proper care in the monastery.

I shudder with trepidation whilst I sit beside Gerard and reflect upon Norah's words, which were spoken in swift, sharp outbursts; it seemed that to speak at all had been physically painful for her, and that her will had been overriding her inclinations. There are certain questions knitted inside my head like a spider's web, along with a very unnatural fear crawling up my spine every now and then, for what lies in my destiny I know not, save for the peril that may soon cross paths with me.

I'll take my own precautions. The rest is up to God.

15

Jayda Pearson's Diary

May 9th, 1903

The terrible memory of that chilly night of May the 7th still hadn't faded from my mind when another incident occurred.

Last night, my husband came to our room in somber spirits and sat down to dinner without relish. Justin was very much concerned about me, for the grisly event had left such a lasting mark upon me that I began to fear the darkness more than anything.

What sat in that misty abyss beneath the bridge will perhaps remain a dreadful mystery for the rest of my life. But one thing I can feel is the coming of some great doom, and I feel many lives are in grave danger. I feel this in my heart.

To let go of any foul imaginations, Justin decided we would go out fishing. It is, anyway, his favourite outdoor activity. I remember him singing like a bird each time we met at the lake before our marriage; he actually proposed to me on a fishing boat!

It was a bright day, and we rejoiced under the warm sunlight. Alleviating westward wind carried the sweet fragrance of fresh water and embraced the region, which consisted of a circular stretch of green in the middle of a large pond beside a wide river, the opulent surface of the water shining like emerald in a glaze. Flooded across the ground and over the banks were rows of shrubs that bloomed flowers of captivating tinct. A very light fog swept across the surface of the pond, pierced by a single sunbeam of bright yellow. The magnetic charm of the scene was such that I considered it must be heaven. My initial thoughts had been of a dream or fantasy, which I often tend to sink into whenever my husband is around me

"I'm so very glad for you, my darling," he said, holding both my hands. "I love you, Jayda," he concluded, and we kissed. I must admit that kissing my husband on a boat is something without comparison.

If my memory has not yet deceived me, I remember it was around fifteen to twenty minutes later when Justin's fishing rod showed tension in the line. An expression of pronounced delight flushed over my husband's face.

"Looks like we're about to reap the fruit of our patience," remarked Justin, winking. I was thrilled too, but my merriment sank back when the tension in the line intensively increased. I could make out by the vigorous frown on Justin's face that things were slipping out of hand.

At first, he tried to sound casual, and repeatedly told me that we'd caught a monster of a fish, but the impression of suspense turned to one of dread as the target struggled closer to the boat.

Justin's face changed, and he held up a trembling hand. I had to assist him to secure both the rod and our boat, for the tug-of-war was so tremendous that it made our vessel shudder. My imagination began to run wild. The fear of encountering a river monster like those in fairytales struck me dumb and froze the blood in my veins.

"We should release it at once," I cried out. I swear upon the holy name of Jesus Christ that as soon as my cry echoed across the pond, things fell immediately under control, as if nothing occurred in the first place. The tension in the line slackened.

I exhaled a long sigh of relief, but as I settled back, I noticed a pair of bitter yellow eyes at the stern of the boat. I gasped, and then the eyes dipped back into the water and disappeared.

It was so flustering and immediate that it left not a fraction of a second for me to react. What I could make out through the opaque surface was yet another mystery, for it wasn't any river monster or a predator. Rather, it was the radiant face of a very beautiful woman, perhaps a fairy or a siren, as heard in the Grecian tales of old. I could study no other feature so quickly, save for a mass of blonde hair. Whatever it might have been under that water, it was remarkably strong and exceedingly fast, for it vanished into the profound depths of the river in the blink of an eye and left not a single trace behind.

Eventually the line tightened again and the target at the end of the hook was but a fish of normal size. My husband, with a dull face, stared at it long and fixedly. Perhaps he was interpreting his own theories in mind to feed his suspicion. I think he was finally satisfied, for he never spoke another word about it. As for me, my mind is rebellious because of all I've witnessed in recent days, and it will never be at peace until the riddles in my head are resolved.

I await the day when Raelyn and I will reunite to share my adventures.

Justin does not wish to discuss the earlier incident at the river.

I tried to speak with him at our dining table, but he simply switched the topic and instructed me not to become entangled in my own imagination. He may term it whatever he likes, but to me it was reality. I saw those eyes. I saw that woman. Each time I recall my experiences of late, my desire to meet with Raelyn grows irresistible.

Justin and I had a hurried dinner and visited the market to purchase a loaf of bread for breakfast. Although a fog rolled over the city in the later hours, the early part of the night remained cloudless, and the streets were brilliantly lit by a full moon. The yelping of a pack of stray dogs could be heard from the opposite lane. People began returning to their houses, save for a couple of gamblers seated aside the narrow lane and who looked in absolutely no mood to return to their wives.

It was only when we crossed the guesthouse where Nathan Connolly slept that an unusual feeling overtook me, for his abode sat in complete darkness as if it had been vacated for ages. Not the slightest flicker of a lamp came from any of the windows, while a horrible stillness in the atmosphere set me on edge.

"He's a scoundrel," muttered my husband, sharing my view whilst we trod. "Isn't he your friend's cousin? I usually find him peeping out through the blinds whenever I cross his house. What strikes me most odd is the way he hides every time he notices me watching him. He ducks behind the wall the way a toddler takes refuge behind his father. I pity the lunatic."

"I fear he is slipping away," I answered. "Raelyn says he is struck with both anxiety and some strange malady of the mind. What else can explain his behaviour?"

Whilst I spoke to my husband, I noticed the singular lane that joined the guesthouse to Raelyn's mansion, and a sudden and queer thought crept into my mind.

Could Nathan have done something to Raelyn? Was that the reason for her sudden departure?

I turned to look again and was suddenly taken aback.

At the far end of the road, swallowed in the grim jaws of darkness, stood a formally dressed man with a large hat and a stick held in his hand. I could not see his face, for he stood outlined against the dim light coming from the houses around him. But what I could make out from a sudden shift of his head was his face draped in what seemed to be a handkerchief. And then, I saw his eyes, which I very well remembered from my return from church. I watched as he began gesturing to something, or someone, near me. I wanted my husband to have a look at this odd man, but when I touched Justin's shoulder and we both looked back, the man was gone.

Good Lord help me, protect me, guide me, and always keep me around the ones I love.

Justin is asleep and again I write. I fear that I might someday lose my mind, for sleep has begun to betray me, while each day shows me new evils that are beginning to affect my life and my safety.

There appears only despair wherever I look.

What is worse is Justin's indifference, for my husband does not see things the way I do. Rather, he is so relaxed after each incident that it makes me question my own sanity. It's as if he believes nothing out of the ordinary has occurred, as though maybe it was only an agitated stray dog down in the mist beneath the bridge, or some great and healthy fish that had, by some miracle, grown strong and large enough to nearly flip our boat.

I often feel like laughing at my husband's idiocy, but that would solve nothing. I perceive only two ways that can lead us out of this desolation. The first is what I'm not sure of, and perhaps would complicate things further, which leaves me with just a singular option—Mark Huddleston.

16

Letter from Raelyn Atherton
to Jayda Pearson

May 11, 1903
Swindon

My dearest Jayda,

You will not believe what I'm about to tell you. Good heavens, I'm still blushing as I pen this letter.

Gerard and I are finally getting married here in Swindon! The thought itself tickles my stomach. I know you must be troubled by my sudden departure. I sincerely apologize for putting you in such elongated suspense. Consider this letter an informal invitation to my much-anticipated wedding. I've waited for this day to come. At last, my patience shall be rewarded. We have a lot to speak about once you arrive.

Father Malcolm has assigned me a crucial task, but to me, it seems that there has been a sudden change in his plans.

He has arranged our wedding before Gerard and I should again depart from one another. Gerard is making a rapid recovery and Malcolm sees this as a perfect opportunity to turn him into a groom.

The wedding shall take place on the eighteenth

of May — exactly a week from this day. Presently I'm too involved in the preparations, and hence I beg your pardon for not being able to respond sooner. Justin and your presence are requested at once, and I insist you leave for Swindon right away.

This is probably the last letter written from Raelyn Atherton, for I shall soon be Mrs. Raelyn Woodward. I love it more than anything.

Here in wait, I shall see you soon. With love and scores of kisses.

Yours truly,

Raelyn

Letter from Jayda Pearson
to Raelyn Atherton

May 13, 1903
London

My beloved Raelyn,

You can never imagine how extremely happy and delighted your letter has made me. Congratulations on your forthcoming marriage to Gerard. You deserve all the happiness in the world, my sweet Raelyn. I can't wait to see you. Justin and I are leaving for Swindon tomorrow morning. We have a lot to share and to enjoy together. I can finally sleep peacefully.

Just a few more hours and we shall be together again. May our reunion be blessed.

Your companion for both this life and the next.

Sincerely,

Jayda

17

Gerard Woodward's Journal (Preserved in the records of Father Malcolm Isaac Simpson)

March 11th, 1903

I feel like crying. I'm perplexed, distressed, defeated, anxious, eviscerated, emasculated, and left to share a terrible fate like that of the servants of this hellish castle.

Lord Ferdinand Elvin Mathers spoke to me no further about my departure from this place. He was rather silent for the rest of the ritual, until the dead servant, Maverick, was buried in the crypt.

Jared's malicious voice still resounds in my head, though he was too stubborn to speak a word more than what he intended. About this man Jared, the wicked butler, I presume that words would never suffice, and also the ink shall run dry if ever his pathetic, mysterious character is to be described. The greatest of writers would miserably fail upon that, and this I can absolutely assure. My examination shows that I am dealing with a cautious and expert criminal.

I often desire to kill him with my very own hands, but I fear the repercussions that might occur. Escaping this purgatory and reuniting with you, beloved Raelyn, is all I think about. It is the only positive thought that has kept me alive here for so long. Every other thing besides it is a lie—a great, big, thumping, obtrusive, uncompromising lie. Any other man in my shoes might have been long dead by now. But my own destiny terrifies me.

I have been escorted to my room and, as usual, have been locked inside to sit by the window. I take in the air with infinite sadness, like some disconsolate prisoner.

But I no longer feel like a prisoner. Rather, I am a goat that has been preserved for slaughter.

I feel like the world has turned upside down upon me. There is an intense feeling in my heart; the agitation within me is so perpetual that moments ago, I was hurling myself against the walls in my chamber.

It isn't just my detention inside this damned castle—to be honest, I have grown used to my imprisonment. Rather, a very implausible discovery has brought me into a state of delirium, where I fancy who my friends and foes really are.

My friends, until now, have been only those of my own blood or those whom I have known a time. But one singular person has changed all that:

Maverick.

Yes, you read it correctly, my dear Raelyn. The servant, now asleep in his crypt.

I found a short message under my bed that was darkly mysterious in drift. I do not know how long it has been lying there, but it was a message scratched by Maverick. The message reads as follows:

Mr. Woodward of London,

You might at first take this as jest or perhaps some other form of trickery, but trusting me is your only assurance of survival in the castle. A single mistake shall cost you your life.

I know that you're somewhat related to the holy Father Malcolm Isaac Simpson, and this is what brings me to your aid to get you out of here safely. The day that you find this note shall perhaps be when I am no longer alive, for Jared suspects my intentions and my wavering loyalty to the Mathers family. I suspect that you've always doubted the butler and that you may possess a very foul opinion of him in your mind. I won't argue in this regard, though I plainly warn you to remain strictly aware of Jared.

I know you have been sneaking out of your chamber at night and exploring the castle to find a means of escape. You may find this surprising, but allow me to confess something:

Who do you think opened the last window into the chamber for you to wander freely within this fortress? I know that you followed Jared into the dungeons. You may well have presumed that it wasn't too difficult to fool the silly servant, Maverick. On the contrary, I have been watching your every step.

You may feel a tinge of longing to learn more about this place and its people, but I am not the right person, and this is not the right time.

You shall be taken out of this castle, but only if you obey me. We will probably never meet again. The day of my death shall be the much-awaited hour of your freedom, for consider it as a signal upon which Darryl shall sneak in and remove you from this nightmare. All you need to do is follow the cloaked man.

And just in case you are unaware, good sir, Darryl is the

cart driver who originally dropped you here.
Forever in the service of Father Malcolm Isaac Simpson.

— *Maverick.*

Had a decent sleep this afternoon, but Maverick's death has disturbed me so much that I awoke with questions swirling in my head.

What if it really was Jared who had killed poor Maverick? Is the butler so threatening? If so, may he eternally burn in hell for the poor, innocent life that he has taken. And of the old man, my heart thuds in horror and repulsion. Is he old and wretched, or is his appearance merely an illusion which he has so brilliantly carried to deceive the world? And what of his daughter? Are there not one, but two daughters whose hands are equally dirty in this terrible game? And the maid Rosa? Is she an accomplice too?

I became obstructed with these repeated questions so fiercely that I began to fear my own shadow. May the good Lord bless Darryl, the odd cart driver, a man I once thought repulsive but who now is my only hope. If we are successful in escaping this place, I shall owe him my life for not abandoning me.

My day was lonely until Lady Helena brought me my lunch—salad, sandwiches, and roasted meat. As much as I hated her, Helena looked more bewitching than ever before. She was in brighter spirits than previous days, which I attributed to the renewed health of her father. She spoke to me in a way of compassion and earnest, and

I could not but humour her in conversation.

She inquired a lot about you, Raelyn, about your career as a doctor (which she found strange but inspiring), your likes and dislikes, about your physical features, your traits, and how we met each other. She insisted I not conceal the tiniest of truths, for she and her family—if they are to be called one—are very happy for us. I noticed that her smile possessed a tinge of bitterness.

"You remind me of my elder brother," she said, taking the bowl from my hand. "Christopher Mathers. He is just like you, quiet and secretive. It has been a long time since we were separated, and I look forward to reuniting with him just like you shall be reunited with Raelyn."

I felt a maddening rage overwhelm me when she spoke about our reunion, Raelyn, for the Matherses are the sole reason why it has been delayed. I wanted to ask about my departure and whether I would ever be allowed to leave the castle and return to London.

"You shall leave the castle as soon as Christopher arrives. It's a promise from both my father and I."

"How long will that be?" I asked impatiently, though she didn't respond.

I wanted to strangle her as she left, but the glorifying thought of Darryl's entry into the castle tonight soothed my heart, and I simply watched her go.

I shall wait in earnest.

It is midnight. My fingers are numb as I endeavor to write. I have, within the last few hours, endured so much.

There was a churn in my stomach as I awaited Darryl's

arrival. As the time passed, I began to doubt he would come for me at all. So, I decided to attempt my perilous path one last time.

I threw my legs over the window ledge and traversed across the row of slabs and, to my dismay, I found the last window sealed. It appeared that Maverick really had been assisting me, but with his death, now there was no one. With bitter hatred in my heart, I began traversing the slabs back toward my chamber.

I noticed an abrupt movement beneath my feet. There, down in the muddled corridors, a ray of light emerged from one end and disappeared in the other. I quickly pressed forward to get a closer view and discovered the woman from the woods, the twin of Helena, blonde hair floating behind her as she walked.

The flicker of the lamp's light upon her face revealed something terrible. There was something unnatural and inhuman about her face, and I felt a chill all over my frail body, for through the gleam of the lamp, I saw the hue of her eyes, a deep yellow . . . like that of some dreadful monster.

I remained fixed to the outer wall and made no movement until the woman passed beyond the window. I felt a flush of relief in my heart, and as my nerves were calming from the close encounter, I felt a sudden rhythm of hot breath upon my neck.

Steadily, and with a hammering heart, I turned around.

Fixed to the wall like some terrible lizard was a figure draped in black from head to toe. The only things visible were its ape-like palms, which were pale and bruised, while a heavy metal chain was coiled around its neck.

I recalled the creature that had escaped through the

window the moment I set foot into the deserted chamber a few nights prior.

The creature shrieked and I suddenly lost my balance upon the slab. I grasped at my stick, my mind paralyzed as my body swung back in the air. All I could think about was the painful moment when my body would hit the hard stone path below and the life within me would finally implode. I fell, and I fell . . .

But just as I was about to hit the ground, I felt a pair of strong arms miraculously catch me. I was right at the brink of collapse, so I couldn't see much of the figure that had suddenly emerged from the dark. He was heavily veiled and swift as air. I thought perhaps I was in the claws of Helena or her villainous twin, or perhaps the vicious ape creature.

But I soon discovered this person was an ally, for as he dragged me toward the gateway, I watched through blurred eyes a quick and vicious exchange between this stranger and Jared, the butler.

Despite my blurred vision, I heard a deep slashing sound, one which occurs only when a blade cuts through flesh. I watched as the butler collapsed and writhed in pain, until he became stagnant, and I was carried away.

I'm quite sure that I must have passed out right after that, for I recall nothing else of the castle. Consciousness came slowly and after a good amount of time, for I woke up in a comfortable bed in a cozy, well-furnished apartment, with two candles burning upon the table and two upon the mantelpiece. Surely, this was heaven.

Before my eyes (and to my great surprise) stood my friend, Ralph Brewer, accompanied by the cart driver, Darryl.

The first thing I was told right after I awakened was

that I was no longer in the castle but in a hotel room in Cardiff. A wave of emotion washed over me while tears of joy flooded my vulnerable eyes.

"Stress no longer, my dear fellow," said Ralph in a tone of condolence. "You are in safe hands now. We shall leave Cardiff on the fifteenth of March."

A slight panic welled within me, and I wanted to learn about the delay in departure. I wanted to be rid of this place forever. But my friend seemed rigid, and I knew that he was worried for me. I comprehend that. Anyone in his place would do the same. My health has strangely deteriorated. I wonder how Raelyn will react to it when I meet with her again.

"It is good to see you again, sir!" said Darryl in his own absurd voice, which now sounded more melodious than a nightingale's song. "You seem to have prominently changed since the last time I saw you. Rest now. Conversations can be held later."

I turned to Ralph, who was preparing a drink.

"Make one for me too, Ralph," I said with a wink. My friend chuckled and placed one more glass on the table.

18

Letter from Ralph Brewer
to Father Malcolm Isaac Simpson

March 13, 1903
Cardiff

Honourable Father,

I write with great pride and gratification that the task you assigned me has been successfully accomplished. Gerard has been taken out of the castle.

I give thanks for the assistance that came from Darryl and the Reverend Sister Marion, who, in disguise of an old woman, managed to stall the cart midway and lent Darryl and me enough time to crawl inside. It makes me fancy, Father, how broad your reach truly is. I respect you for it. I always will.

Raelyn will be so delighted to see Gerard again. Though his feeble health will undoubtedly scare the life out of her, I know that her love for him is beyond measure.

I also admire your great intelligence, for your strategy to sneak us into the castle worked fruitfully. The cart was filled with bread, meat, wine, fruits, and vegetables of various kinds. Darryl, due to his slim build, was able to hide inside the fruit trunk, while I had to take shelter under the seat.

Something chilled my bones then . . . the mingled whimper of what sounded strangely like infants I heard coming from a trunk beneath the driver's seat. An intense feeling of rage weighed heavily upon me, and I wanted to investigate the matter. But to fulfill my duty, there was no other choice but to suppress my desire and remain crouched where I was.

Darryl told me that the cart driver is the only servant permitted to bring provisions into the castle. No other person is allowed for that errand. Though, I suspect there had also been a lady with him in the front, for despite the darkness, I saw the thin, pale hands of a woman gripping the reins and riding horseback. I fear she is a confederate in some sort of dark practice which I know not. But what terrified me far worse was the thought of my dear friend, Gerard, and how he survived for so long in such a repulsive place.

The castle grounds were crowned in a dreadful silence, and I felt sickened at heart as the cart approached the gates. An unnatural fear, one which I had never ever experienced in my entire life, came upon me at the first sight of the towering edifice. A weird stillness sat upon the place, and no sound—not even the slightest of whispers— came from the enormous stone structure.

Standing under the arched, open gateway was an army of servants, huddled together like a flock of sheep.

The woman on horseback hoisted a heavy bag over her shoulder as she climbed down, and with a little assistance from the man beside her, the couple and all the servants disappeared into the gloom of the castle.

I knew it was the perfect opportunity for Darryl and me to emerge. It was quickly decided that Darryl would stick around the cart and keep watch while I ventured inside to look for Gerard.

Fortunately (and also miraculously), I found my friend somewhere I would least expect: balanced against the exterior wall of the castle and upon a row of protruding slabs, his gaze fixed below on a figure holding a lamp in hand, walking through the passage. I moved forward to get a better view of the person. But as I did so, the figure suddenly disappeared, as though plucked away into the darkness of the corridor.

Then, suddenly and dreadfully, a terrible dilemma forced me to step out of the gloom and into the open, to run to my friend's aid before he met a terrible end.

What I saw from far below was an enormous ape-like creature descending the battlements and about to pounce upon Gerard. The immediate arrival of the monster left both Gerard and me panic-stricken, and my fellow, as a result of sudden fright, lost his balance and fell like ripened fruit from a tree. Here I acknowledge my quick reflexes, for I caught Gerard in my arms before his body could hit the cobblestones.

When I righted myself and ensured we were both alive, I glanced up at the battlements, but to my awe and disbelief, there was no sign of the creature anywhere.

There wasn't a moment to lose in idle imaginations, and hence I rushed towards the singular walkway that led outward to where the cart stood. It must have been a slight mistake of ours that a butler spotted our intrusion and blocked our path. I had Gerard over my shoulders and perceived no other way than to kill that miserable man with a knife I had hidden in my waistcoat.

Darryl appeared right in time to drag away his lifeless body so that we might escape unnoticed. With my friend Gerard Woodward laden over my shoulder like a sack of rice, we boarded the cart. Darryl climbed into the driver's seat, whipped the reins, and spun the horses 'round.

Fate favours the brave, Father. We successfully managed to break out of the castle and onto the road to freedom.

Sister Marion has instructed us to stay in the hotel until the term appointed. I received your parcel this morning, sealed with your strict command rather than glue, along with firm instructions not to unpack it before the fourteenth. I believe that I shall know the truth at the proper time.

Until then, Father, rest assured I will take proper care of my companion.

I'm still confused whether the path of religion is truth or delusion, but I feel relieved to have helped a person in need. If this is supposed to be the purpose of our existence, then I'm happy to be a part of it. The only thought which troubles me is the affliction that has fallen upon Gerard during his stay in the castle.

Humbly awaiting further instructions. For friendship and for love.

Sincerely,

Ralph Brewer

19

Gerard Woodward's Journal (Preserved in the records of Father Malcolm Isaac Simpson)

March 13th, 1903

I feel dizzy and have spent most of my time sleeping. I haven't seen Darryl since I woke up, but Ralph has been quite busy at his table, staring at a sealed box from Father Malcolm and scratching notes, which I find odd. I've known Ralph for ages. He is as much repulsed by writing as he is by religion.

I pray that he finds the correct path to save his soul from humiliation on the day of judgement. I fear it is coming soon.

March 14th, 1903

Had a long conversation with Ralph. He seemed eager to know about my stay with the Mathers.

I wished to display my journal to him, which, I believe, has much more to say than my tongue. But, it often crosses my mind that I've poured my heart inside this journal, which I want none before you, my beloved Raelyn, to ever read.

I'm aware that my words inscribed in these pages shall worry you to an extent which I may never fathom, but I'm quite sure that your love for me will grow stronger after we meet. I consider myself lucky to have defeated death and escaped the torment of hell with the assistance from Ralph and Darryl, and of course Maverick, whose debt I can never repay.

Though, I wonder why poor Maverick kept such secrets from me. I firmly believe that together, we might have shed light to certain mysteries lurking inside that castle.

I offered my gratitude to Ralph. He, in return, pretended to be courteous. In actuality, he seemed perturbed by some queer thought in mind that had, in the least, pushed him to the verge of impatience. He is the sort of man who is more accustomed to using his muscles than his wits.

What troubles him so much I know not, but I feel a sharp spasm under my flesh that tells me that I shall have many things to write about in the near future.

───────────◈───────────

I feel as if I haven't slept properly. My eyelids droop heavily, but each time I close my eyes, the horrific moments spent in that desolate castle haunt my eyes, sending a paralyzing fear through my spine and all across my body. Sleep eventually disappears.

One thing I know to be true is that I would have gone mad had I not had my journal to express my suffocating heart. Ralph has generally been out of my sight for most of the night, save for earlier this evening when he accompanied me for a cup of tea. He once again set out of our room with his parcel, and I haven't seen him since.

Darryl has again abandoned us, and I might never know what became of him.

Whenever I flip the pages to write, I feel soothed and secured. It is my strength. I shall lie down and think about you, Raelyn, about the moments that we are going to spend together. I must stop here, for not every secret needs to be revealed, though I cannot help the satisfactory smile upon my brooding face.

I think I shall finally fall asleep.

Christ help me! I feel as if I'm on the verge of an apocalypse, for what my eyes have just witnessed is proof that Hell itself has come to the earth.

It started with an innocent dream. I saw myself walking the streets of London, the thrill of which was so intense and saturating that it made the last flickering of my sorrow fade away. I was so delighted by the majestic scene of my hometown that soothed my eyes and restored my soul with her fresh air, fragrance, and elegant charm.

While I walked and thought of you, Raelyn, I saw a cat standing motionless, glaring with intrepid yellow eyes that were struck with a spark of ferocity. She reminded me of the castle, where I witnessed the vicious jaws of a similar animal. Whilst I proceeded further down the lane, the cat eventually disappeared into the dusky gloom.

My heart suddenly burst with joy and anticipation when I heard the whisper of the woman I love. Yes, it was your voice, Raelyn, your harmonious voice that possesses the gift to heal my suffering heart. I swear upon that. Fortunately, the woman with that euphonious voice belongs to me, and I to her. A thousand praises to Almighty God.

There came a rapid surge in my adrenaline upon hearing your voice, and as I turned around to respond, the location in my dream had instantaneously changed, as if by magic.

I found myself standing on a wooden bridge that connected two granite crags at a remarkable distance. A giant river flowed beneath the bridge, sending a shiver down my spine whilst I struggled to maintain my balance. The farther end of the bridge before me was misty and dreary, and made the courage within me run dry. But as I turned around, I felt a flush of merriment to my spirits, for I saw you, my love, standing at the opposite end. There was not a shadow of doubt about the choice I would make and, without wasting a fraction of second, I staggered across the bridge in your direction, Raelyn, to touch you, to kiss you, to hold you in my arms and never let you go again. I wanted this longing to finally end.

The bridge was suddenly tossed by a violent wind. I gripped the rope and resumed the trek, and just as I was about to cover the petty gap that separated me from my woman, there followed an atrocious tragedy. The violent shuddering of the bridge plucked the dusty rope, emitting a loud crack, and the bridge collapsed. The tremendous horror of the incident happened in a blink of an eye, and as my body tumbled down towards the river, I awoke.

I felt a heavy weight upon me as I returned to reality. And as I looked up, I saw a pair of vicious, baleful, yellow eyes charged with utmost malice, set firmly behind a repulsive face messed up in tangles of chestnut brown hair.

It was Helena, her cold breath beating upon my bare skin.

The door to my chamber suddenly flung open as Ralph barreled in with a pointed object in hand. I thought it to be a crucifix at first, but Ralph's attitude toward religion made that thought fade right away. Then followed a terrific tussle between my friend and the woman creature. Any living person might have guessed that Ralph would dominate the brawl, but things were exactly the opposite. My friend could not withstand the great force with which Helena struck him every single time, and eventually the object slipped from his hand.

I noticed that it was an antique dagger of some bygone era.

Ralph struggled to grab the dagger at any cost, and his sore expression spoke of his helplessness without the weapon. I was weak in every limb, but still wise enough to make a choice as to what I must do.

Abandoning Ralph to Helena's hands was my only chance to grab the dagger. It was a splendid chance of opportunity and would serve as payback for all the sufferings that I had endured as a prisoner of the Matherses. Nothing would soothe my wounded heart save for retribution.

I myself would kill Helena Mathers and her devil father.

With surging hatred in my heart, I lunged to my feet and reached for the blade. The moment I grabbed hold of it, Helena's strong hands grasped my shoulders, and I was immediately thrown to the opposite corner of the room. There was something abnormal and misbegotten in the very essence of the creature that now faced me. I was still trembling with shock when a fresh horror struck upon my soul, for I had by now lost sight of Ralph and presumed myself to be the sole victim lying vulnerable before the fiend.

She pounced upon me like a predator and held me down under the gigantic strength of her palms. A moment of stillness sat between us as she choked me. I slowly and steadily slipped away under the grip of death.

But then, I heard a swift slicing sound, like a sharp autumn wind raging at dusk.

I was deafened by the horrible squeal that followed, the pitch of which was so sharp that I felt my head spin. Ralph had stabbed Helena right through her heart.

The evil woman loosened her grip over me and writhed in pain until she finally collapsed to the floor. Right in front of our eyes lay the body of a woman sorely contorted and still twitching. My final vision of Helena Mathers—the creature known as Helena Mathers—was her body crumbling like dust and evaporating into thin air.

My hand trembles both in relief and shock while I sit and pen down the night's events. It is over. I believe it. I know it.

If the world around you is evil, you sometimes need to shake hands with the devil. I only wager about the old man and how he will react to his daughter's death. I hope he finally dies with the tremendous shock, a shock that no father in this world should be able to bear.

If this is war, then let it begin.

Letter from Ralph Brewer
to Father Malcolm Isaac Simpson

March 15, 1903
Cardiff

Father Malcolm,

I write this half dazedly but with an enlightened heart. May you always remain safe and bound to serve humanity. Things I have recently witnessed have, in the very least, made me question my lack of faith in things outside my control.

To be quite honest, I'm desperate to talk to you.

The task you set for me has successfully been accomplished. It was Gerard who helped me kill the fiend. As you mentioned, Father, the fourteenth was a new moon. Darkness conquered the farthest end of the territory and I, despite my impermeable heart, withdrew the crucifix that had earlier been affixed to the bottom of Gerard's bed whilst he slept. I never thought this little piece of wood and metal could possess such enormous propensity to resist the dreadful creature I had to later kill.

Gerard was suspicious of your parcel. Believe me, Holy Father, I never let him unbox the contents, which I blasphemously called the enchanted dagger. I regret my profanity, for now I refer to it not as enchanted, but sacred—it was the only means of stopping that devilish woman. I washed the blade in holy water and took care of all that you have instructed me to do.

The woman whom Gerard calls Helena Mathers has died, and we've moved to the secret location, just as you

116

have commanded. Sister Marion and Darryl are in touch with us. We further await your orders.

I see a ray of light before me, manifest though diminishing, and I want you to guide me towards it.

Forever indebted to Darryl, Sister Marion, and you.

Faithfully—if this ever suits me,

Ralph Brewer

Telegram from Father Malcolm Isaac Simpson to Ralph Brewer

March 17, 1903
Newport

It is appeasing to hear that you've felt changes in your faith. However, it's always the great God who needs to be praised, rather than a mortal human being like me. I'm on my way to Swindon. Get there at once.

—Malcolm.

20

Jayda Pearson's Diary

May 19th, 1903

Swindon is beautiful. God is great!

Raelyn and Gerard are now bound by the sacred bond of marriage. I'm delighted and overjoyed. Occasionally I smile, ponder, and blush at the thought of my beloved Raelyn, who must finally be so happy.

Time in Swindon flies by very quickly, for it has been around a week since our arrival here, and now I have finally found time to return to my diary to write down my thoughts. I did not realize it then, and now I sit and wonder and bloom. Prior to the wedding, Raelyn and I giggled for days, as neither of us ever fancied just how well our husbands get along. It amazes me but shocks Raelyn. She's so innocent and sweet; I adore her beautiful face. She and Gerard are a perfect match for each other.

The wedding happened yesterday. It took place before a small congregation in the great hall of one of the protruding corridors of the monastery, with parallel doors and illuminated stairways that, quite swiftly, expanded towards the dungeons like the spreading wings of a hawk. Following the dungeons, the path leads to a sealed gateway, nailed with a thousand scriptures of black and white, which to me appears quite bizarre, for none other than Father Malcolm has the authority to enter it. Every other resident is confined within the boundaries of the dungeon.

As Raelyn has lately been sequestered with her new husband, and Justin has been out with an old schoolmate residing in Swindon, I had no other choice but to roam this place. Though, I do not regret my decision, for in the very least, it has given me something to write about.

I feel hungry after such a long morning.

I'm in the dining hall and awaiting lunch at my table. Waiting makes me impatient and so, I write. What bothers me at present is a woman at the far end of the hall who attempts to stare at me and get away unnoticed. What she fails to perceive is that I'm Jayda Pearson; it's remarkably difficult to spy on a woman like me. To me, she looks as proud as a peacock, lean-faced, grey eyes small and twinkling, as if constrained with lunacy. She is taller than she appears, with traits of an aristocratic maiden who is far too occupied with her own self. Each time I glance at her, she seems to act in a strange manner, as if awaiting someone to share her nothingness. How pathetic.

I can scribble notes on her perpetually, if ever I choose her as the subject. But thank heaven, my lunch has arrived, and I am starving.

Goodbye, strange lady, and do not look at me again.

I'm startled.

I was out for a walk by myself due to Justin's absence, thinking about loneliness. Loneliness is what I fear most. It makes me wonder why on earth poets prefer to remain alone, lest some fortune may fall and the ink in their pen runs dry. If loneliness is required to compose poems, I'm quite happy as a housewife.

Upon my return, I had a brief conversation with Father Malcolm. He is adamant, spiritual, enthusiastic, and insistent. Such a personality can resurrect so much faith in any infertile heart; I've absolutely no doubt about that. Speaking to him has not only consoled me but has also strengthened my grip over my own faith.

Just as I retired to my room and was about to sink into this diary, I found an anonymous note upon my table. It made my stomach churn.

I've attached it to my diary below:

Mrs. Pearson,

Please do not trouble yourself over this petty note, for there would only be failure in any attempt to disclose the identity of the correspondent. What is of utmost importance is the purpose for which this note has been left on your table.

I'm sure the first person that comes to your mind after reading this is the poor woman in the dining room. But trust me, Mrs. Pearson, that you watched her for no appropriate reason. She was just an ordinary woman, awaiting her food like yourself.

This brings me to Justin. I'm certain your husband won't be returning any time soon. I want you to leave him a letter regarding your sudden departure and speak not a word about it to anyone else. This departure not only regards the questions buzzing inside your head, but includes a certain past that has always haunted you. I hope you haven't forgotten your dear, departed father.

Now, make haste. I shall await you at the train station.
A slight reminder—come alone.

I awaited Justin for hours. My heart is on fire. I feel dizzy, perplexed, and somewhat impatient about the contents of the anonymous note.

I wanted to see Raelyn before I left, to disclose this little piece of paper, to ask her valuable advice. But she has hardly stepped out of her private chamber since the wedding. It reminds me of my own wild passion after my marriage to Justin. It's human nature. I understand that.

I've left a small note for Justin at my study table, and now, as my cart approaches the station, my mind is rebellious. I no longer have the audacity to bear such intense anticipation, which bears heavily upon my soul. I don't know whether I have made a wise decision or a terrible mistake. I do not know if I will ever return.

But, as far as the secret to my father's disappearance is concerned, everything is worth it.

Raelyn Woodward's Journal

May 19th, 1903

I feel so blessed. Finally, I am his wife. Mrs. Raelyn Woodward.

After another long night, my husband is asleep. I wished to accompany him, but I don't feel the need to sleep. Instead, I'm about to head to my darling Jayda's room. I know she will be eager to gossip about my first night as a bride.

Hold on Jayda, I'm on my way.

Christ, show me a way. Jayda's room was deserted and there was no sign of Justin. I think Justin must have taken her out for dinner. I've always appreciated and admired the bond between the two. A perfect couple. It's often made me jealous. But I love Jayda, and she deserves nothing below the mark.

Discovering no sign of her, I retreated from her door. There was a vague thrill in my heart to rush back to my husband, but as I stood on the threshold about to push open the door to our private chamber, a sharp voice called out to me. With a sour feeling of interference, I turned around and found Norah walking towards me.

"Father Malcolm reminds us there isn't a second to waste," said she in a low but resolute voice. "We need to hit the track."

"Now?" I protested. "First allow me to say farewell to my husband."

She shook her head in quite a strict manner. "You cannot."

"Why?" I queried immediately, feeling a twitch of exasperation.

"Because he isn't alone inside," she answered. I threw a bitter glance at her, but before any word left my mouth, she spoke hastily. "Your husband is having a conversation with Father Malcolm. He seeks no interruptions and has ordered us to take our departure at once. Pace up, Mrs. Woodward; we have a long road to undertake."

As we sit in our bustling cart, I struggle to figure out what Norah meant by her warning. If this really is a lengthy track, perhaps with no point of return, then I want you to know, Gerard, how much I love you.

I can never describe it in words. It's like the deep murmur of the ocean, perpetual but refreshing, bearing in it, along with the breeze, the fragrance of the sea. I hope someday we shall sit together on the sandy shore, hand in hand, murmuring with the echoes of the wind and rejoicing over the glistening sand. We won't be in a hurry and there won't be any external interference. Just you and me. Together. Now and forever.

If there is any peril in the path I take, may the good Lord take away my life and breathe it into yours.

21

Notes from Sister Marion Baynham (Preserved in the records of Father Malcolm Isaac Simpson)

September 7th, 1896. Cambridgeshire

It is this second case which has chilled my heart with dread. Unlike the first victim, who died right at our arrival inside the chapel, this person remains in very bad health. I must take proper care of him until Father Malcolm returns from his expedition.

Day 1

The victim is remarkably fragile and shivers pathetically. It seems as if his soul has already escaped his body in small proportions, for the red seems to have gone from his lips and gums, and the bones of his face stand out prominently.

The man who brought him appears to be an insoluble person: lean, curly-haired, with crooked fingers and a sly looking face that seems to fold within itself a hundred mysteries. I remember the name he told me. He is Maverick. The victim's brother.

I pity the poor fellow and pray that his brother recovers.

Day 2

The victim's condition seems to have stabilized. Though his haggard face bears an expression of some great disaster, he breathes soundly. He can open his eyes, and he sheds tears at the sight of his brother. I feel as if he wants to talk. But his body, unfortunately, does not possess enough strength to speak. He needs rest.

Day 3

To my astonishment, the patient's health has drastically deteriorated, and it looks to me as if this is the last day of his life. His dull, protruding eyes are constantly fixed upon the ceiling. May God bless the poor soul and grant his helpless brother the strength to bear the loss.

Day 4

I have now begun to doubt my very own conscience, for again, astoundingly, his health has shown improvement. His face, which was until now as white as a sheaf of parchment, had restored some of its redness. He is still not in a condition to speak, but gracefully pointed a finger to seek a glass of water. I'm glad, but also shocked, for the bizarre fluctuations in his health have left me puzzled.

What I have observed so far is his sleep, for he tries vigorously to avoid it, and he only gets worse each time that he sleeps. I might be wrong in my assumptions, but there is currently no valid theory to draw conclusions upon his case, until he is medically examined.

Day 5

Alas! The patient has died. I'm perturbed, and despite

the furnace, I quiver against a cold that has iced the marrow of my bones.

The patient's medical reports have been presented before my table, and I see there was an immense drain of blood and semen from his body, which further resulted in the decrease in blood platelets and finally, a failed heart. Now I perceive why this man suffered from fatigue and was incapable of movement. His body seems to have lost all its elements, bearing resemblance to a barren field that hasn't experienced rainfall for years. May his soul rest in peace.

His brother, Maverick, is nowhere to be found. Perhaps he has deserted this place, and I daresay he won't be a part of the funeral. May the Guardian Angel have mercy upon him and grant him strength to endure the pain.

September 15th, 1896

Had quite a long conversation with Father Malcolm, the priest who arrived just last night. He disclosed a bitter truth that left me to fall back upon my chair:

The patient and his brother, Maverick, also had a sister, Brianna, who committed suicide last year. It was due to the unnatural death of her newborn. The young mother claimed to have regularly fed her baby and yet, the innocent life was lost as a result of starvation. She was devastated and decided to end her life too.

"The catastrophe that was, at a point in time, confined solely within Cardiff has now crossed boundaries into different territories," confided Father Malcolm. "I fear there is a strong accomplice behind it. Someone who is dangerous in the extreme, but also, the least likely suspect."

His voice raged like a sharp bell in my ears, leaving

me in blatant trepidation and exposed to all sorts of foul imaginations. I wonder who the evil culprit is, and how far the shadow of death has spread.

"I want you to visit Cardiff," commanded Father Malcolm at last. "Darryl has received all my instructions and he shall assist you there. Also, Maverick has pledged vengeance and swears to be a part of our holy cause, to stop this evil and help spread the word of God to every corner of the world."

I inclined my head thoughtfully and listened. He continued, "We need to remain extremely cautious and await the right opportunity to strike. Each clue that I have gathered during my investigation leads to nowhere but Mathers Castle. They are the last of the species that remain from the royal blood. Darryl is constantly writing to me, and I want you to be a part of it.

"A new victim will likely be targeted sooner than later, and that is the perfect time when we shall strike. Until then, what we need is patience."

September 19th, 1896. Cardiff

Cardiff is marvelous. Endearment is the first impression the place has left upon me ever since I left the train, for as my cart crosses any street or locality, the unique charm bewitches me.

I ponder whether the things I previously heard about Cardiff are anywhere near the truth or mere idle gossip blended with lies and assumption, twisted by knaves and fools to knit tales of lore around the fire. I never would have believed any of it, had I not myself been witness to the patients, or if any other man besides Father Malcolm told me.

His words burn inside me, for if the reality is so ugly here in Cardiff, I fear everything here is a delusion.

It was a wild, cold, seasonable night, with a pale moon lying on her back as though the wind had tilted her.

At the end of my journey the cart stopped, and I was helped down by the gentle driver, who I confess appeared to be a man of sinister disposition. He introduced himself, and I was astonished to learn that the cart driver was Darryl himself. He is a man with limited speech and only opens his mouth if there happens to be an issue of utmost importance to address. Besides that, he hardly talks or smiles. His habits, from what I made out during our first encounter, seemed simple to the verge of austerity.

Darryl helped me with my luggage and escorted me to my room in the chapel. I see him as a religious person, for his actions speak of his devotion to Father Malcolm. I had quite a delicious meal served at dinner, and now, as I sit at my table, I feel sleep overpowering me. I need to stop. Morning shall be a fresh start.

I am excited and determined to resume the Lord's work.

22

Raelyn Woodward's Journal

May 21st, 1903

I don't know which part of England I currently tread, but there is a pinch in my heart. This place has seen evil. I sense that a foul secret is buried here.

When we arrived, a beautiful view sat before my eyes—small houses, orderly and well-constructed, brick-red in colour, with narrow lanes and structured pavements, bordered by an enormous moorland to the north and connected to a cluster of county roads.

Norah had stuck to silence for a prolonged period, and only after entering her town did she trouble herself to speak.

"If God consents, good lady, you shall now learn about the horror that stirs every heart in this place," she said to me. She led me straight into one of the houses, which consisted of a well-furnished room with a wooden shelf occupied with antiques, a small table laden with scrolls, and a glass of wine that lay untouched by the fireplace.

I was introduced to Johanne, a simple yet peculiar woman. She was similar in age to Norah, save for her flushing cheeks and an accent which, if I guessed correctly, spoke of her French ancestry. It appeared that Norah had already spoken about me before my arrival, for Johanne seemed very formal and pronounced my name in quite a friendly manner.

I was seated beside the furnace, and Johanne displayed before me a bundle of scrolls, most of which were addressed to the nuns in Cambridgeshire. The rest seemed to be notes, which were inscribed in Johanne's own handwriting and told of a tragedy that surrounded their remote town.

"What is it that haunts the womenfolk here?" I asked.

No words came from her mouth. She stared at me bluntly, as if I was some culprit who had just confessed her crimes. Then there came a sudden change in her bearing, and holding her breath in a state of agitation, she responded, "Children."

I sat back and listened with intent.

"We've been witnesses to such things that one would never believe. I command you to remain patient and see it with your own eyes. I want you to notice the fear and agony that resides here in many of the women's hearts.

"Maevis was a sweet, innocent young woman. Lovely too. Not as much as yourself, but pretty in her own disposition. It was after a period of six years that her first child, a girl named Marie, was born. You can imagine the boundless love that must have aroused the woman's heart.

"But what equally shattered her heart was the death of Marie after less than a week. The infant died as a result of starvation. Maevis could not bear the shock and lost her mind after her baby's demise. What troubles me most is what she said on the day of Marie's burial."

"What did she say?" I stammered.

"She said she left Marie sleeping in the cradle and moved to the other room to tend to her husband. She heard a sudden, unusual sound, rushed to her infant, and was petrified to find Marie stuck to the wall like a lizard. She gave a horrible cry and collapsed, and the next thing she remembers is being awakened by her husband on their bed. Some might call it a nightmare, but she swears it was as close to reality as the moon and stars. She had never given a thought as to why her baby had stopped weeping all the while, and after a couple of days, the poor child left the world. Many other women have similar stories. They fear and complain about their dreams—delusional, but at the same time, as real and as true as their bearing."

I listened eagerly and with a faint heart. Despite being a doctor by profession, I can only imagine the dread that poor Maevis must have felt at seeing something so savage, even if it was indeed a nightmare. I pity the woman.

I shared a cup of coffee with my new companions and together, we spoke of other queer cases that have shaken the village.

I may not always be brave, but I'm resolute, I'm somewhat stubborn, and above all—I have the Almighty, and He is all I ever need.

May 22nd, 1903

The day is nearly reaching its end, but I haven't come across anything strange, save for idle talk. Women are highly talkative, and they chatter about for hours and hours. I myself can be a part of it, but only if Gerard is the subject of the conversation.

One thing I've observed about the people of this town is their wide consumption of onions. It gives me the impression that their recipes rely solely upon onion, or that the meagre population here is fully capable of collectively eating half the onions in Europe! When I inquired about it, Johanne told me that it was Sister

Marion who recently insisted upon it, and that they have grown quite accustomed to it.

Strange!

May 23rd, 1903

Our third day here is about to pass, and still no incidents. Norah seems embarrassed. She avoids making eye contact with me. Johanne invited me over earlier this evening, but she too had not a word to speak about. Rather, she chose the topic of my wedding while we emptied our glasses.

I pray that Father Malcolm is taking note of the situation so that I'm returned to Gerard as early as possible.

The people are beginning to whisper that their misfortune has passed away with the arrival of Mrs. Raelyn Woodward. Women look to me as a saviour, or to be more appropriate, a blessing in disguise.

I'm no different than them—mortal, sinful, permeable, and repenting. I only look forward to my return to London so that Gerard and I may start this new phase of our lives.

May 24th, 1903

Yet another day is about to end and gracefully, there hasn't been anything bizarre reported. People here are overwhelmed with delight. I'm happy for them. I've written to Father Malcolm explaining the situation, seeking his permission to return to Gerard.

The only thing I can do is await his reply.

I'm agitated and numb. My body shivers in horror.

As I was lingering on the verge of sleep, I sensed the presence of a shadow trailing across my window. It looked so real, as if I was standing there to watch it pass along the mist. Suddenly, I bolted awake and sat up with a horrible sense of fear and emptiness inside me. I remained motionless and vigilant, and then I heard a harrowing whisper pass through my room. What made the noise I know not, but the idle talks of the womenfolk echoed inside my head.

Quickly, I rose to my feet and opened the door.

It was a beautiful night. Stars twinkled in the sky, surrounding the moon like the subjects of an empire assembling before their queen. A cool breeze swept the land. I inhaled a long breath to ignite the fire of courage in my heart, and without wasting a moment further, snuck away towards the south, where I again heard the whisper.

The town veiled its florid charm and lay comparatively empty of passage. There was no sign of any living creature as I strayed from the tracks and entered the vast moor. It was a vivid space of silver and brown, flooded till the horizon.

My eyes caught a glimpse of two lean figures, tall and cloaked, slinking towards what seemed a maze of tall hedges. I took the opposite route to counter and confront them. Fervently I chased the muddy track, occasionally peeping through the hedges to take note of my (and their) position. Finally, our paths merged into a common track. Ready to face the peril that was about to confront me, I stood blocking the maze's exit.

The figures emerged and became paralyzed upon seeing me block their path. I maintained the upper hand and higher ground.

"What do you want?" I yelled.

"Forgive us!" pleaded a male voice from behind his hood.

I ordered them to lower their veils and, surprisingly, saw that they were a young couple—a boy and a girl on the verge of adulthood, who had obviously developed a passion for each other. The young love birds shuddered with fear, constantly beseeching me to keep their liaison confidential and far from their parents' knowledge.

I offered a fair trade and only gave my word once the couple promised to answer the questions troubling my mind. I asked them about the happenings in their town, along with a detailed account of events which Norah and Johanne were too confined to share. I wanted to know the truth, piece by piece, and warned them not to conceal the smallest portion of it.

The lass turned white to her very lips as she answered. I shall try to write down as much in her own words as I can remember:

"Mothers of Malton fear their own children at night," she said. "It might sound strange to you, good lady, but we hear and witness things. Terrible things. My mother says to avoid going too far, especially after dusk. Infants die quite frequently, while womenfolk often commit suicide or become chained by their own mental disabilities, which to me is a far greater torment than death."

"Hear, hear," I agreed.

She spoke of one such victim, Rebecca, a plump, red-headed woman who mentioned that her baby seemed uniquely beautiful one night. After a while, when she returned to the room to look upon her sleeping child, she was petrified to find her boy sitting cross-legged in the cradle, staring at her with a malignant smile and rigid, bright yellow eyes that shone in the dark.

"Just think of it, good lady. Simply imagine the fright that must have seized the poor mother. Her husband failed to see what she was witness to, and the child died a couple of days later. Rebecca hasn't spoken a word since and sheds her tears in isolation. There are many other cases like Rebecca's. The only help that came before your arrival came from Sister Marion. She ordered us to consume onions with every meal. Also, the mothers of infants and toddlers were ordered to place onions in every corner of their house; I heard my mother speak of it to her friends."

She mentioned that this method prescribed by the devoted nun had worked fortuitously, for the harrowing case of yellow eyes had never again been reported in Malton. Rather, the disaster changed its form, and children began to go missing at night. At least, until my arrival in town, which led to the abrupt, unpredictable, and miraculous passing of the calamity. Nothing had been reported since.

"May the good Lord bless you for it," she concluded, and I noticed tears leaking from her green eyes. I had no other choice but to let them go. Though, I certainly warned them not to land themselves or their families in trouble with mere acts of childhood lust and stupidity.

As I was about to head back to my cottage, I noticed a violent movement behind the bushes, which stiffened my spine with fear and unease. At the far right of the maze, I saw a very ugly face glaring at me in a fixed stare. The face was dark, hairy, menacing, and possessed the sparkling yellow eyes of a demon.

Suddenly, the face vanished into the mist.

I stood for a few minutes with my heart in my boots, wondering whether the whole thing was an elaborate hoax. I quaver miserably as I write this, for I think that what I saw was an ape. An ape in the moorlands! Ridiculous!

Despite being at ease right now, I'm sure about one thing:

Sleep won't be returning to me anytime soon. I know that in my bones.

23

Letter from Father Malcolm Isaac Simpson to Sister Marion Baynham

May 27, 1903
Swindon

Devoted Sister,

I would once again advise you to be extremely cautious, for what I've suspected is becoming, part by part, a certainty. The reason for sending Raelyn with Norah proves that.

Raelyn hasn't witnessed anything peculiar during her stay in Malton, which piques my curiosity, for silence is evil's most destructive weapon. I need to figure out why the servants of hell have remained dormant in her presence.

It's certainly concerning and needs to be sorted with courage and wisdom. Be in regular contact with Darryl. Keep me updated with all that happens.

Malcolm.

Letter from Ralph Brewer
to Father Malcolm Isaac Simpson

May 31, 1903
London

Honourable Father Malcolm,

This is solely to bring into your kind notice that both Raelyn and Gerard Woodward have returned to London. For them, a new phase of life begins; and as for me, I'm determined to undertake any perilous path for your holy cause. Your company has not only brought my soul out from the dark, but now I see the purpose of my life.

I shall forever be grateful to you.

In service to humanity and religion,

Ralph Brewer

Letter from Father Malcolm Isaac Simpson to Ralph Brewer

June 2, 1903
Swindon

Dear Ralph,

It's quite a pleasure to witness the change in your character. Here again I shall mention that nothing happens without the will of God, and that it is He who should always be praised.

Darryl can act on his own. Your presence in London is no longer needed. Return to Swindon immediately. I have important things to discuss with you.

Malcolm.

Raelyn Woodward's Journal

June 2nd, 1903. London

It's good to be back home. I feel the refreshing winds of London kissing my cheeks and gently brushing my hair in salutation.

Gerard is in high spirits too, and I take immense pleasure in assuring, by his solitary countenance, that my husband won't be leaving London anytime soon. God, the thought thrills me to the depths of my soul.

We also stopped by Nathan's doorstep to greet my cousin, but he never answered. His door, which was equipped with neither bell nor knocker, was blistered and distained. His window drapes were layered with dust.

I would have transferred Nathan Connolly to an asylum long ago, had it not been for his awfully deficient health. I'm well aware that he won't get the proper help and attention there, and neither would he get any better in prison. I fear he would rather die. I never want that to happen.

"We shall tend to him shortly after we have peacefully settled," proposed my husband in his usual affectionate tone, and we returned inside our cart.

———————————————

Gerard pities Nathan. I noticed a look of disquiet over his charming face as I told him the series of Nathan's incidents. I also told him about the sudden and unpredictable weakening bond between myself and my cousin, as we had grown up with love, affection, and respect for each other. My husband wore a look of stern sadness. He promised me that he would eventually speak to Nathan and do everything in his power to fill and mend the gaps in our relationship. How sweet of my husband. We had an intimate conversation at tea, after which Gerard parted to meet Mr. Anderson for some purpose related to his profession.

I was at my study table with my favourite volume of

anthropology and a glass of wine. Whilst I was drowned in the contents of both, a terrible scream burst from the silence of the night. That frightful cry turned the blood in my veins to ice. It came from the posterior of my house, which opens to a small lawn, a tree, and a storehouse in the corner. To my great distress, the stony path cutting through the lawn was dotted with droplets of blood. An agonizing fear sprang upon me as I chased the bloody trail until, at the end, I saw something that made my head spin.

A butchered cat hung lifeless from the tree. Her stomach was ripped open, her dead, yellow eyes staring coldly at a point in void space.

I found no trace of the intruder who had slain the cat.

I'm frightened to conclude this in such a way, but whoever was behind this inhumane act seems more like a possessed, wild beast than a man.

June 3rd, 1903

Last night's incident left a lasting mark upon me. I spoke to my husband about it this morning. His teeth grinded together, his face rigid and fearful to hear of my account.

He kissed me and took me in his arms, asking me more than a dozen times if I would be all right. Only after becoming fully assured did he let me go, eventually rising from his chair, retiring to our bedroom, and returning with a revolver in hand. I insisted that he should keep it for his own safety, for his profession demanded it, and that he shouldn't stress about me. But Gerard is stubborn. He told me that he had another revolver to care for himself, if ever things slipped out of hand, and this revolver would now only belong to me.

"Keep this for the sake of God and do not leave home after dusk, Raelyn," he said. "There's a savage creature walking loose on the streets at night. I've heard people's complaints about their animals being killed. The police have undertaken the case, and whatever the creature, it shall be shot on sight."

My husband's words echoed in my ears, and unable to bear it for long, I decided to visit Jayda. But here awaited another shock.

Jayda's house was locked, the curtains drawn. I wonder where in the world she is, and why she feels the need to roam.

Does she not know of the danger?

June 4th, 1903

I returned to my clinic today. I feel relieved taking care of the sick. It reminds me of the preaching of Jesus. It gives me such blessed satisfaction that I can carry on my work for ages without halt.

It was Thursday evening when a lady named Miranda, a middle-aged, fair, and intelligent woman, arrived with an unremitting mark of sorrow on her face. I came to discover, after a long consultation, that she was suffering from sleeplessness and emotional defeat.

"My husband Peter and I have no children after five years of marriage," she grumbled and occasionally lowered her voice to suppress a sob. "Casper, our dog, was the only thing dear to our hearts. He was our only means of joy and laughter. It happened a few days ago when Peter and I decided to go out. Casper was resting in the hall, and my husband did not want to disturb him. It was very late when we returned, only to find Casper ripped to pieces. His body had not moved an inch from where we remember to have left him. Blood was all over the floor, and it was so appalling that I fainted. The whole incident has ruined my relationship with my husband. We hardly share a word. His silence is what kills me. I'm troubled with it to such an extent that I have not eaten, and I fear my health has begun to deteriorate.

"I need your assistance, doctor, in rebuilding the bond between Peter and me. Please cure me with medics, if required, so that I may carry his child, for I hide this disability of mine with an almost morbid sense of shame. I beg you to help me. I shall be ever grateful to you."

Miranda broke into tears at last, and it took a great deal of time to finally console her grieving soul.

"Miracles do happen," I reminded her, patting her back. "Nothing is impossible for God. Have faith and take proper care of your husband. Give him the pills which I have prescribed and report to me after a week. Spend a good amount of time together and talk about the things that interest you both."

There was a mark of satisfaction upon her face as she left my clinic. I only pray that I can help relieve her pain.

The only worry that remains in my heart is this fierce predator that preys in the dark. If the police ever miss him, I promise it will be me who slays the beast.

Gerard Woodward's Journal

June 4th, 1903

I write with great anxiety, affliction, and dread that my wife was left alone with a savage creature that tried to break into our house. Esmé, our domestic cat, was savagely mauled. I won't ever be able to praise you enough, Lord, for saving Raelyn.

I did not want to add to my woman's fear or worries, but I have warned her not to leave our home in the dark. Of this bloodthirsty creature, I swear that I myself shall slaughter it, if ever again it happens to cross my path or comes within a mile of Raelyn.

This brings me to Father Malcolm, who has taken from me a major part of my journal which narrates my days in Cardiff. I wonder if my writings will ever be returned to me, lest they be shown to my wife.

June 5th, 1903

Raelyn appeared so marvelous today as I kissed her goodbye before departing for work.

The breezy curls that frame her mesmeric face, the bewitching charm of her magnificent eyes, the delicacy of her roseate lips, her dazzling teeth. Every minute detail comprising my wife's beautiful features are impossibly heavenly. I confess that Helena Mathers was extraordinarily, abominably, and dreadfully beautiful, but the charisma of my beloved Raelyn is unmatched.

While I was still enthralled and fascinated by my wife's beauty, my cart abruptly came to a stop, lurching my body forward like a storm toiling a boat in the sea. The driver's bitter words reached my ears first, and as I peered through the drapes, I noticed a stringy figure crossing the road, ignoring the cart driver's yells. The man hopped a little distance ahead and shrank back with a hissing intake of breath. The look of him, even at a remarkable gap, went somehow strongly against my inclination. He was pale and gave an impression of deformity. I thought he would return, perhaps to brawl, but rather he threw a sharp glance, both at me and the driver, and disappeared into one of the lanes.

As I was about to pull back the drapes, a sudden feeling of awe and loathing struck me. I had seen this stranger before . . . if not his face, then surely his structure. I regret not recalling the appropriate place and time, but I'm sure I had seen him before.

My day proved to be tiresome, and as I was walking home with an enlightened mind and an eagerness to reunite with my wife, my eyes fell upon the guesthouse of her estate. Nathan Connolly's residence. It appeared that the place hadn't been inhabited for some time. It was filthy, abhorrent, and somewhat in ruins compared to the charm that it once reflected. Despite repeated whispers in my ears not to proceed any further, I decided to investigate, if only for my Raelyn.

A thick layer of dust rose into the air as I knocked. No response came from the other end. I knocked once more, called out to Nathan loud and clear, but still no answer. I raised my glance towards the upper window and noticed a spider's web stretched around the frame. I gave a final knock, this time harder than before, and though no voice was heard, the door squeaked on its hinges and opened with a creak.

A very foul smell burnt my nostrils and almost made me expel my lunch. Pressing my handkerchief over my nose and mouth, I entered Nathan's home that bore resemblance to a tenebrous cave in the middle of a dark forest. Amongst the cluster of passages, dirty scribbled walls, dusty floor, and ruptured ceilings, there were numerous sacks piled one after another in a corner of the hall.

I was crestfallen to see patches of blood spread all across the furniture, which now seemed to be the habitat for termites and worms. I could hardly believe my eyes to see the pathetic mess this place had become. A feeling of repulsion mingled with fury came upon me, and with intense vexation, I moved upstairs.

Nathan's room resembled a chamber of hell. The pungent smell grew unbearably strong and choked the life out of me. The room was as still as a graveyard, with piles of notebooks and papers, a horribly dirty floor, damaged walls, an unkempt bed, and a destroyed cupboard. The slight beam of the streetlamp entering the drapes was the only light to diffuse the darkness within.

I scanned every corner of the hellish room to locate Nathan.

Suddenly, in an untidy corner and shrouded in the dark were a pair of small, piercing eyes, shining like sharp metal exposed to fire. Staring at me.

I started back in such a manner that my hand hit hard against the ruptured wall. Here, something sprang upon my back and I, struck with fear, lost my balance and rolled down the stairs, hurting my legs and elbows in the process. The breath was knocked from my lungs, and only after coming to a stop at the bottom of the stairs did I realize that rats were crawling all over me in Nathan's den. I wasted not a second more, jumped back to my feet, and with a firm grip of my stick, left the guesthouse and staggered back to my home.

Now, as I sit in my room with a mug of coffee, and after lying to my wife about how I obtained these bruises, I promise that neither I nor my wife will ever visit Nathan Connolly again.

I fear what my wife's cousin has made of himself.

I fear more about what I'm going to tell her.

Raelyn Woodward's Journal

June 6th, 1903

Gerard was injured last night. My heart was in agony to watch my husband suffer. He says he slipped while getting down from his cart. I'm afraid he is not speaking the truth. I shall try to convince him to speak when I take him to bed. Perhaps that is where the truth will come out to play.

June 7th, 1903

I confess I was chasing the wrong track, for what my husband told me of his injuries seems true. He said nothing different when I asked again as we lay entwined in our bedsheets.

Today, I started early and visited the church, which has not only revived my spirits but has also encouraged me to weigh down my scale with good deeds. Upon my return, I stopped at Jayda's home. It is still locked. I wonder where she is and what she is up to. I wish she had spoken to me before her departure.

Come back, Jayda, for your friend desperately awaits you. Life is strange. The more we try to comprehend it, the more complicated it becomes.

June 8th, 1903

I'm in tears, grieving, baffled, addled, demented. My poor heart feels stabbed with an everlasting wound.

Gerard and I had a long conversation last night. Things were so beautiful and intimate in the beginning. He then proceeded to share with me some of his adventures in Cardiff. It was so frightening and unpredictable that I felt chills all over my body.

"This is exactly what Father Malcolm, too, must have discovered through my journal," he concluded at last, smiling with an air of embarrassment which, I presume, was a brilliant attempt to conceal his dread. "I have brought upon myself a punishment and a danger that I cannot name."

"It is all over now," I replied, and kissed away his worries. He agreed with a constrained gesture.

Our conversation brought to memory the little secret that I had, until now, kept hidden from him. I decided to finally disclose it to my dear husband. Confident as I was that he would not trifle with my appeal, I laid the truth before him.

It was a dire mistake, for the moment I spoke to him about the disappearance of Jayda Pearson's father, a terrible change fell over Gerard's face.

I never saw in all my life, in good and in bad, Gerard stare at me in such distress. His face turned white as chalk! I noticed him shivering, evidently torturing his mind about something, but he never spoke a word about it. Instead, he abandoned me in the hour I needed him most and set out with his luggage. The only thing he said was that he was leaving for some very important work and that he had no idea how long he would be gone.

I don't know whether I have broken his heart with my secret, or perhaps it is he who is concealing a much larger secret from me.

Great Lord, please have mercy on me. I beg of you to set this right and bring my husband back to me.

June 10th, 1903

Two days have passed, and I am lonely. It feels as if everything was a dream—a beautiful, ravishing, seductive dream, one that has finally ended, and now I awaken to the ugly reality of life.

My heart burns. My eyes constantly shed tears. I'm in extreme pain and yet there is not a soul to lend me a shoulder to weep upon. This must be punishment for some sin that I have committed in secret or in the open, knowingly or in delirium.

If this is supposed to be my end, I only pray, merciful God, to not make me suffer any further. Make death swift and easy upon me.

June 14th, 1903

More days have fled and still no news from Gerard or Jayda. I have written to Father Malcolm and Ralph, and yet no response has come from either. I feel broken, shattered, drowning in the bottomless depths of depression.

Unable to bear this torture any further, I set out for

church this morning. The once-bewitching glamour of London felt pale and perishable as I walked. Nothing was pleasing to my eyes; neither the neatly dressed revelers on the road, the elegant ladies and gentlemen, the radiant sun overhead, the refreshing winds, nor the rows of beautiful houses.

The only place that enlightened me in my state of misery was the church.

I confessed and prayed and cried and begged for God to absolve my sins. I finally felt so relieved that I spent most of the day sitting idly in the front row.

Darkness had returned by the time I got home. I hoped I would be welcomed by my husband upon my return and, hitherto, I started and turned towards the door with a face of expectation, but a wave of hopelessness and sorrow overtook me when I realized Gerard was still gone.

What I did find, however, was a small gift—neatly packed and addressed, laying untouched on my doorstep. There was an anonymous note attached to it that read:

Dear Mrs. Woodward,

My apologies for not writing to you sooner. I was stuck in unavoidable circumstances that caused a delay in presenting you with your wedding gift. Congratulations on your marriage to the man you love. I pray all the happiness in the world is granted to you, and may you and your husband, the esteemed lawyer, stay together forever.

You might be eager to know about me. You must only know that I'm one of the names closest to your heart.

24

Letter from Sister Marion Baynham to Father Malcolm Isaac Simpson

October 3, 1896
Cardiff

Honourable Father Malcolm,

It is a matter of great privilege to write to you now, for I take immeasurable pride to inform you that our purpose has fruitfully been fulfilled.

There are many things I wish you to know. Let me begin with the simplest:

Maverick has passed the test of Lord Mathers' loyalty and is now one of the servants of the castle. Evil has its own ways, Father. Trust is the base ground of both evil and good; Maverick's trial has made me realize it. The Matherses do not trust any living soul without serious consideration.

Whilst Maverick was involved in earning a place at Mathers Castle, I came across three more deaths under similarly horrific circumstances. Peter was the name of the third deceased, who, though initially admitted as a patient for a period of three days, seemed to lose every drop of blood from his body, until the grace of death showed mercy upon his soul. What I could study during this short interval, which to poor Peter must have felt to last for ages, was a swift change in his bearing, followed by a rapid decline in his health while at rest.

I had been told of his taste and preferences, and yet the poor fellow developed a strong repulsion to onions. Once, he became a victim of food poisoning when Sister Felicia secretly mixed it in with his lunch.

His words, which he spoke to me on the night before his death, still haunt me. It was evident that his dreams had manipulated him:

"I won't get any better, dear Sister, I know it better than anyone," he mumbled, struggling vigorously to breathe. "I would only be deceiving myself to think or believe otherwise. Aye, I know that I'm dying, and that you should be cautious of my state of delirium regarding whatever I have to say.

"But it isn't just a dream, Sister, believe me. It is more real than sleep. Flowers are beautiful for a butterfly until it encounters a mantis disguised as one. I see moonlight, hear a nightingale's song, feel the fresh wind, and chase starfish in a very opulent pond. But I eventually wake up, breathless and exhausted. In my dreams, I see a heavenly damsel walking around me like a fairy in some enchanted forest. I feel her more than I feel myself, but again I awaken. I feel tired, I get discharged, and yet my inner self craves sleep more than ever before. I feel a very strong chill in my heart when I try to sleep, for as I grow drowsy, I see a baleful sparkle of yellow eyes in the gloom, which tranquilize me with something I can neither see nor express. I fear it, but at the same time, I need it.

"I will die, Sister, I will die. And that shall be fortunate for me."

I choked with emotion when he finally died. His words left me in such distress that I've developed a foul reputation of every person, living or dead, here in Cardiff. Sister Felicia also fell sick to an unknown malady, but thank heavens, she hasn't fallen allergic to onions, unlike my earlier patients who are now resting under soil. She shortly returned to her initial strength. It is a most queer case.

I've had a brief discussion with some of the residents. What I've learned so far about the Mathers family is as little as a shell dropped on a seashore. They are an ancient race that stem from a time when the war to unite England was at its peak. They were resilient and immovable and adjusted their lifestyle from luxurious to laborious and back again. The Mathers family also played a key role in the war against Napoleon Bonaparte. Some say they lived about a decade in the forests without proper food and water.

An elderly man in town, called Jonathan, proclaims that Lord Ferdinand Elvin Mathers isn't the father to the so-called daughter, Helena. Rather, there is a very dark secret that bonds them together. What it could possibly be, no one knows. Jonathan swore upon his faith that Lord Mathers has only one child—a son, Christopher, whom no common eyes have ever seen.

His words terrify me. I spent a great deal of time speaking to people individually, but no new useful information unraveled.

That is, until, one night during the final hours of the gloom, right before the dull grey of dawn, I heard a knock at my door.

It was an elderly woman, around five-and-sixty years of age, resolute but choleric. She was strict in her manners and firm in her speech. This might sound strange, Father, but despite our long conversation, she never revealed her name and kept her identity confidential. I did not know her initial intentions, but her words have cleared the clouds of mystery in order to better understand our foes.

I shall try to write her exact words as far as I can remember:

"Believe me, Sister," she said. "I bring to you the naked truth. Children and men are dying in this town. Mothers often complain of their newborns. I'm sure you have heard men speak of a melodious voice echoing in the woods. What I'm about to say might be known to some as myth, which makes me choke with laughter, for they are foolish to think so.

"What brings death to this place is a Xana. If she is not stopped, her reign will expand uncontrollably. The Xana is a creature of extraordinary beauty, believed to live in fountains, rivers, or forested regions of fresh water, though they are highly adaptive to change and will press their boundaries whenever vengeance is concerned. Their hypnotic voices are more often heard during spring and summer nights.

"Those who call a Xana beautiful might only judge a pond by its surface and have no idea of the dreadful face beneath. The Xana possesses large, yellow eyes like those of a wolf. It feeds on blood and semen, can swim at a remarkable speed, can breathe underwater, and avoids the sunlight to maintain its strength. The Xana cannot feed her own baby and hence, secretly exchanges it with the child of a townswoman. This child will appear exactly as the townswoman's own, and she will feed it new life while the Xana feeds on the mortal child.

"The Xana's only known weakness, written in books of old and passed from generation to generation, is her strong repulsion to onions. Though onions cannot kill a Xana, they are an offense to practicing their dark arts. There is no record on its method of reproduction, and its survival is as strange and mysterious as a thing could be."

I noticed a struggle within my elderly visitor, and despite her collected manner, she appeared to tremble, as though wrestling some type of hysteria.

I feel that her information could prove to be a gateway to open certain doors that have, until now, remained locked. I'm aware this information may help us learn how to counter this great catastrophe, but I fear the obstacles in our way can neither be prevented nor foreseen.

I need to learn more about the woman in the castle. Though presently, I perceive no possible way to do so. Perhaps Maverick might prove to be of some assistance. Patience will be required until fortune favours us, which, I believe will happen soon.

I will continue to explore every minute detail relating to Lord Ferdinand Elvin Mathers and his legitimate son. I shall remain consistent and promise to write to you immediately, if anything comes to light.

Forever devoted to service for mankind.

Yours faithfully,

Marion Baynham

25

Letter from Ralph Brewer
to Father Malcolm Isaac Simpson

June 17, 1903
Bristol

Reverend Father,

I consider my time spent in Swindon to be the most valuable and precious hours of my life. A pathetic, blasphemous, miserable disbeliever like me has been granted the treasure of religion. I shall ever be grateful to you for it and will follow your teachings to the best of my ability.

Ralph Brewer is no longer an agnostic.

Gerard Woodward has arrived at my place. He is anxious, swayed with anticipation, curious, and struck by agony he does not wish to admit. I don't know what troubles him, but he seems determined to revisit Cardiff. I presume he has either lost his mind or gone astray by paying heed to the devil's whispers.

I am stuck between friendship and restriction. I ask for your guidance at this difficult time and to help me make the correct decision.

I shall be highly obliged to you.

Sincerely,
Ralph Brewer

Letter from Father Malcolm Isaac Simpson to Ralph Brewer

June 20, 1903
Swindon

I knew it would happen one day. Delay your expedition for a period of three days. Start your journey on the morning of the twenty-fourth. Also, be extremely cautious, as Darryl won't be a part of your next adventure.

Malcolm.

Raelyn Woodward's Journal

June 14th, 1903

I feel both like crying and tearing things apart, for a violent rage within is driving me insane. Gerard has still not returned. Jayda is gone too, which brings me to the anonymous gift left on my doorstep.

I now know who left it, for inside the box was an antique vase, which I perfectly remember to have seen in my cousin Nathan's room. If Nathan Connolly thinks he can warm my broken heart with a mere gift and by scratching an anonymous letter, then he is very much mistaken.

I won't ever accept his apology until he personally meets me and explains everything in proper detail.

Until then, his vase shall rest in my storeroom.

June 17th, 1903

It was another strange day for me, save for my time spent in church. The ringing bells, mingled voices of the choir, the elegant candles, and every other thing is a remedy to my soul. I'm an honest Christian woman and I want no treasure of the world as a replacement for this peace.

As I left, I caught a sudden glimpse of Mark Huddleston, sitting on the stone bench in the cemetery and gazing leniently at the sky. He had remarkably changed from the last time we met.

He is not at all easy to describe. I observed there was something wrong with his appearance; something displeasing, something downright detestable. As soon as he became conscious of my presence in the cemetery, the ill-mannered, lanky fellow rose to his feet and fled the scene without a moment's pause.

Why did he not wish to see or speak with me?

June 19th, 1903

God, please forgive my sins, and please save me from this hellish life I can no longer bear. I feel the very essence of my soul fading away. I feel that I may die at any moment, though I believe death might be a relief for me.

The night was reticent. It was the darkest night I ever witnessed in my life.

I arrived home late from the clinic and decided to take a hot bath. I had an enjoyable dinner and then I moved to my study table with a glass of wine. An hour after midnight, I had a knock at my door. It seemed ludicrously inappropriate to call at such an hour that, for a moment, I stared in silence.

I cautiously approached the door, for a voice inside my head suggested it might be Gerard. I tried peeping through the keyhole but found no sign of a visitor. I was resolved not to answer. There came, however, a second knock as soon as I turned my back to the door. A terrible fear fell upon me as, with a thudding heart that pounded vigorously beneath my bosom, I gripped the knob, counted to three, and pulled it open.

There was no one there.

I sealed the door and returned to my work. After half an hour, I rose from my chair and proceeded to my bedroom. A good amount of work had left me craving sleep, something I had been longing for quite some time.

As I began to doze, a lean shadow trailed across the window. Horrified, I grabbed a heavy candelabra and slowly I approached the windowsill. I threw open the curtains, and I saw nothing.

I took a sigh of relief and was not yet done blaming my sanity when the loud shattering of glass fell onto my ears. I screamed and witnessed a scene so appalling that it chilled every bone in my body. The glass door had been broken, and out of the shifting, insubstantial mist leapt a terrible fiend.

It was quicker than a wink and more horrible than death, a human figure crawling like a reptile — nimble, agile, and quick, crawling through the hole and invading my private chamber. I had seen nothing more savage, more appalling, and more hellish than the satanic face that glared at me with utmost hatred.

It was Nathan Connolly.

He had a displeasing smile and there were patches of dried blood all over his grisly face. His teeth were sharp and smeared in red and yellow, his eyes bloodshot, his nails long and untidy like that of a vicious carnivore, and he possessed an ugly, putrid tongue that constantly licked the corners of his mouth.

I started back with a terrible yell and, half-dazed, I dropped to the floor. I tried calling him by name in order to stop him, or to establish some form of conversation, but it appeared as if human language was no longer known to him. He stared at me with hungry eyes, compressed his teeth, snarled like a violent stray dog, and showed every minute sign of a man possessed.

He pressed forward, perhaps eager to tear me limb from limb. I began to lose my consciousness, my vision blurred, and I awaited the savage beast to tear me apart.

But then, my bedroom door flung open, and Jayda Pearson leapt in like an angel from heaven. Her presence not only made me regain my strength but gave me a resolute reason to fight.

Nathan turned his eyes on Jayda, and despite his beastly appearance, his fragile body was knocked asunder by my best friend. As Jayda fought him off, I moved to the glass door and returned with a large wooden splinter. Nathan suddenly overpowered Jayda and held her down, his bloody jaws less than an inch from her throat. I then loped forward and pierced the object into his back. He screamed like a wild boar and lunged at me. By this time, Jayda had returned to her feet and hit him hard with a table lamp.

Nathan dropped to the floor, but rose instantly, like a serpent ready to strike. He tried vigorously to throw himself on top of Jayda, though she managed to cross his hands behind his back and swung him around. I stooped down, grabbed a shard of window glass and, shutting my tearful eyes, I slit open his throat.

Jayda pushed him away and together we watched him spill his blood all over the floor. He stared angrily at first, but then his face softened, and a look of gratitude came to his eyes. I cried. I saw my cousin beneath the monster then, and it broke my heart.

He dropped to his knees and then onto his stomach, and he moved no more. A prolonged silence followed which was marked by nothing more than the distant barking of a dog. I turned to Jayda and saw her drawn, white face, a mingled look of terror and sadness fixed upon it.

"Justin is no more," she finally said with a husky and broken voice, and it broke my heart as much as slaying Nathan Connolly.

I glanced at her and was astonished to find Jayda's features devoid of any expression. And then, a maddening rage of retribution shone upon her face. It blew a similar spark of vengeance in my heart, but was quickly extinguished with a single, terrible thought that suddenly crossed my mind.

What about Gerard?

June 21st, 1903

Following Nathan's quiet funeral, Jayda and I broke into the guesthouse where Nathan had been living, which was a horrible mess of filth and darkness, choking us with its repugnant odour.

There were sacks piled one upon another, bloodstained and containing the remains of dogs, cats, rats, and insects. What became evident was the truth, for there remained not the slightest doubt that the beast that had been preying on the streets of London was none other than Nathan Connolly. I wondered how he managed to evade the police.

I asked Jayda a dozen times about Justin and his unnatural death. The only thing she told me was that her husband had drowned in the Thames and that his body was found a week later in Bristol. I noticed a constant fury that had permanently settled upon her once beautiful face, her eyes filled with hatred.

"I shall not grieve until Justin's death is avenged," she said as she proceeded upstairs.

Jayda has formed quite an obscure image in my mind. To me, she appears to be a woman of knowledge, aware and well acquainted with worldly issues. I'm afraid that she knows many things but conceals them from me, and judging by her grimace, I don't think she will reveal them to me anytime soon.

Nathan's room was terribly destroyed and stank of decay, with broken furniture and walls webbed in ink and blood. I observed many papers dumped around the furnace that I assumed he intended to use for kindling. They were notes from Nathan Connolly, and as I read them, I noticed the constant mention of Mark Huddleston and of a woman named Maria. My cousin was apparently madly in love with her.

Jayda frowned at the name of Mark Huddleston. Upon reading, we came to discover that the Huddleston had presented Nathan with an antique vase, a vase the woman called Maria had thoroughly loved.

Jayda inclined her head thoughtfully as we read, but she never spoke a word. It gave me the impression that she comprehended the situation more than I could imagine, but refused to share it with her closest friend, though I wonder if she still perceives me as such.

I came to a scroll at last, one that left me in an ocean of tears. It was penned by my cousin and read as follows:

Dear Raelyn,

You might think that I've changed to an extent you'd rather not fathom. I'm sure you must have lost all hope in me. I shall never blame you for it. I myself would have done the same if I was in your position. It's destiny, my sweet cousin. It's written. We need to accept it.

I apologize for every single time I broke your heart, Raelyn. If I am the chief of sinners, I am also the chief of sufferers.

Know that nothing is dearer to my heart than you and Maria. She is the only secret that I have ever kept from you. I wanted you to meet her in person, but I felt a flush of regret and shame that stopped me every single time I tried to introduce you. Besides, Maria was also hesitant to meet you.

I might be looked upon as a dull, insane, atrocious creature, but know this, my sweet Raelyn, that Maria is the reason behind it. A man might never be called a lover until and unless he adapts to the changes that his woman desires.

You hold a special place in my heart, my sweet cousin,

and I beg you to forgive me for every pain I've ever inflicted, knowingly and unknowingly, upon you.

Perhaps I will be gone by the time you read this scroll. My only wish is that you remember your cousin, Nathan Connolly, with a good and pure heart.

Yours forever,

Nathan

I was still grieving over my cousin's final note when Jayda came across a terrific revelation. Together, we stood at a point behind the furnace that opened to a deep tunnel that dropped down into a terrible darkness.

I threw a stone into the hole, and after a considerable gap, it clattered on stone. It gave me a chill to follow suit, but Jayda was rigid in her decision, grabbed a lamp, and descended into the hole. I had no other choice but to accompany my friend to whatever fate she was leading us into.

Thick layers of mist blotted my vision. I had no idea where I was going. With suppressed anxiety, I followed Jayda as she hustled along with the lamp held high in front. There came a point when we stopped and stood frozen, staring ahead in silence.

We stood before a web of rugged paths, and each led in a different direction. We undertook a few different routes, and to our surprise, discovered that each opened onto various streets of London.

We now know how Nathan has been hunting all these nights in the dark, and how he has evaded capture. Jayda and I have only one common question left to answer:

Who the hell is Maria?

————————•————————

Letter from Ralph Brewer
to Father Malcolm Isaac Simpson

June 29, 1903
Cardiff

Reverend Father,

I had no earthly idea how ugly the truth can be. I feel dazed. I'm about to disclose such a secret that none but Gerard has known for ages.

He claims to be witness to a grim and horrendous incident in his boyhood, where a man (whom he later came to discover through his wife happened to be Jayda Pearson's father) was slain in the woods by a mysterious woman. He says that she was hooded, and that only her golden hair was visible to him. He was too young to remember any other feature.

His face, as he spoke, was very white and grave.

Before arriving in Cardiff, Gerard insisted I accompany him into the forest, to the scene of the tragedy that he believes is the origin of all his troubles. I cannot deny I wanted to see it for myself. I daresay it was a dark and contemptible place, interwoven with looming trees of brown and green. A stream flowed down the slope, crawling about like some great snake amidst the silvery outlined path of crags and boulders. A firm silence lay upon the woods, save for the burbling of water against the rocks and the crunch of dry leaves under our feet.

We came upon an ancient cave. It was this spot where Gerard remembers to have witnessed the dreadful scene. I can only assume the horror that must have sprung upon an innocent boy, for the revulsion of such a place could make an adult shudder.

Gerard said he had lost his way while playing with his friends, and that was how he came to this haunting discovery. He led me into the cave, and through the flickering light from our torches, I saw a perpetual row of skeletons nailed to the walls. The hair on my head stood up like a hedgehog's quills.

With our hands gripped firmly over our crucifixes, we traveled the narrow path deeper into the cave. We walked a remarkable distance but never found another exit. An unbearable odour of decaying meat cut through our nostrils and felt to have punctured our lungs. We then paced in reverse and left the aggravating abyss. I admit that we ended in failure, and that we were highly disappointed when we arrived in Cardiff.

We might never know what was at the end of the tunnel, but you are a man of true nobility, Father, and I disclose this case so that you may share your wisdom. Please send your valuable advice so that we may end matters here in this land of evil.

I shall await your response.

Faithfully,

Ralph Brewer

26

Jayda Pearson's Diary

June 30th, 1903

I abandoned my diary long ago and never thought to turn its pages again. I never put my experiences into words ever since leaving Swindon. Secrets are sometimes a protection against hazardous threats that are not revealed.

It was Darryl, one of the loyal men serving Father Malcolm, who wrote the anonymous note to me after the Woodwards' wedding in Swindon. We met on a train while returning to London. What he revealed to me was another unfolding in this great and dark mystery. It was none but Darryl, the shaggy man veiling his face with a handkerchief, whom Justin and I had seen a few times watching us in the streets of London. It was Darryl who informed me about my husband's secret trip with his schoolmates. Alas, my husband met his fate and left his soul in the Thames.

I could never have borne this trauma with such great courage had my fate not led me to Sister Marion Baynham, who not only disclosed the truth about Justin's death, but also guided me to take further measures to combat this great evil.

The truth is this:

My husband was killed by a Xana—a term I intensely hate, for it was the same pathetic, loathsome creature who killed my father, a horrible tragedy that has always haunted me.

I spent much time at the monastery, and that was where I came to learn about Nathan Connolly's possession by the Xana. I then began to fear a possible attack on my dearest friend, Raelyn Woodward. I came to learn about certain properties of this loathsome creature, and it became clear in my mind. It was the same creature I had seen in the pond, sinking away into the abyss, those big yellow eyes staring up at me.

Revenge is my right. I will not reach my end until it has been fulfilled.

The challenging task which I have been set is to find the son, Christopher Mathers. God, please let me find him and let me kill him.

Letter from Sister Marion Baynham to Father Malcolm Isaac Simpson

October 11, 1896
Cardiff

Honourable Father Malcolm,

I write to you this final letter from Cardiff. I will soon be departing per your orders. I do not know when I shall return, but I take pride in giving you a brief account of the entire situation in Cardiff.

People here often talk of seeing a beautiful woman in the woods after dusk. Men speak of her peerless beauty, and despite her lucid charm, no man has ever been able to chase her, for she disappears into the trees like some phantom doe. One thing that everyone agrees upon is that the mysterious woman has never been seen during the day. She comes swiftly like a fog at night and passes over like wind in the morning. The crone says that the woman is a Xana, and I too share her opinion. Of this I have no doubt, for each property of the Xana is duly fulfilled by this woman of the woods.

Together, we've unveiled a dark secret confined within the stone walls of the castle. Lord Ferdinand Elvin Mathers has no daughter, and his only son is believed to have left him a long time ago. I often feel the urge to visit the castle in order to seek the truth, but no outsider is allowed in without the old man's consent.

Among the townsfolk here are disgraceful people who have pledged their lives in the service of Lord Ferdinand Elvin Mathers . . . and his gold.

The crone and I buried ourselves with books and scriptures, met hundreds of legends at their deathbeds, traveled to every corner of the land (save for the castle), and did everything in our control to extract any piece of information about the Xana.

Two of its other properties that I have come to discover have left me questioning reality. First, the Xana resides in and travels instantly through ancient and enchanted pots. Second, its infectious bite transmits its properties to its victim. I feel a burning desire to study the bite and to learn every minute symptom in detail, but I shall soon be departing from Cardiff. Hence, I leave this task in your custody, Father. I cannot help wondering what the antique pots must look like, and how severe her bite to a victim can be?

"Ferdinand Elvin Mathers has sold his soul to the devil," said George Burns, one of the men I met early in my quest. "He is a Satanist who sacrificed his wife for a most evil cause. His son inherited much of his father's traits but is believed to be far more dangerous. No eyes have ever seen him, and I can bet you anything that the fiendish son uses this to his full advantage, in order to move freely among us."

Upon asking the prodigious son's name, Burns answered, "Christopher Mathers." Then a drastic change came over his face as he glanced at the window. Struck with awe and disbelief, my companion and I turned quickly towards the window and noticed a shadow bounding away into the trees, like some great ape. We chased it immediately but ended in failure, for the track led us to a large stream and the frightful howling of wolves.

I confess that I haven't made any progress since, and my mind weighs heavily upon my failure. I regret to have let you down, Reverend Father, but finding Christopher Mathers is the only way to stop this devastation.

A great war is ahead, and I pray to the good Lord to grant victory to the righteous.

In devotion to religion and to God,

Marion Baynham

Raelyn Woodward's Journal

July 1st, 1903. London

I've grown accustomed to an acute feeling of being watched by a pair of devilish eyes. I have become more and more uneasy in my sleep, moaning and tossing and turning. I feel an intense glare upon me whilst I doze. But each time I arise, there is nobody there.

Nathan's death breaks my heart, and I still find it difficult to admit that he is no more. May his poor soul rest in peace.

July 2nd, 1903

I was holding my cousin's gift in hand, and as I examined its unique and delicate artwork, the vase slipped through my hands and hit the floor. I was surprised to find that it did not break. I observed the vase closely but found not a single crack anywhere on its polished surface. It increased my wonder. Alas, I believe I was merely fortunate.

I must be careful next time so that Nathan's gift is not wasted.

July 3rd, 1903

I'm in such pain. My anxiety is at its peak as I sit by the furnace after dressing my wound.

My life is shaken to its roots, sleep has abandoned me,

the deadliest terror sits with me all hours of the day and night. I feel that my days are numbered.

I have no idea whether my recent ordeal was real, or if I have finally lost my sanity.

I left my clinic with a vivid and newfound intention to serve humanity. There had still been no word from Gerard, but I decided to remain patient. It was around ten by the time I left. Fog slept above the city, which appeared deserted. I was confused, for even the churches were empty. The lamps in the mist glimmered like garnets, and through the muffle and smother of these fallen clouds, I was hit by a mighty wind.

I walked onward towards my home, perturbed by a sickening feeling of being watched. I came to a point where I slowed down and watched, for through the faint shadows casting through the mist, I noticed the dark outline of a small child chasing me in utmost haste.

I halted with a thumping heart and turned around immediately to help the child, but there was not a soul in sight. I resumed my walk. And then, for a second time, I heard small, childish footsteps approaching. I turned around and again, I saw no one.

I rushed home, and just as I reached the doorstep, I heard the horrible wail of an infant coming from my house, so pathetic and agonizing that it left me rooted to the doorstep. With a deep breath, I opened the door and walked straight into the hall. There was no sign of an intrusion, and things were exactly as they should be.

As a doctor (and from being in a relationship with Gerard so long), I have perfectly developed the ability to observe minute details, where even the slightest misplacement of a lamp does not miss my attention.

The cry ceased the very moment I stepped inside. An

empty wine glass and my favourite volume of anthropology lay untouched at the table before the furnace. The ticking of the clock and crackling of the fire left behind by the maid echoed through the silence.

As I grabbed a lamp, I heard it again. The infant's cry came from upstairs.

I crept up to my chamber and stopped dead on the threshold. There before my eyes and upon my bed was seated a fair maiden with her back to me.

She was golden-haired, dressed in elegant fashion, and holding something against her breast. The baby, from what I could see, was healthy and fair, and despite my initial terror, a speck of relief came over me at the scene of a mother feeding her child. Perhaps it was just a woman off the streets, seeking a place to nurse her baby.

But my solace became revulsion, for as I took a step further into my chamber, the infant slipped off its mother's breast. It leapt upon the bed, and I swear to the heavens that my mortal eyes witnessed the newborn latch itself upon the wall and begin to scuttle like an insect. It shot me a yellow glance and disappeared through the window, leaving me half-dazed, in shock . . . and alone with its mother.

The woman slowly turned her head.

I felt the breath leave my chest, petrified as I gazed upon a devil incarnate living just beneath the delicate skin of the mother. Her eyes were yellow, like some dreadful serpent, teeth jutting out of her drooling mouth like a starving wolf. Her pale skin was nearly translucent and revealed the veins and arteries beneath.

Never had I felt so close to death than when I encountered this vile creature, her mere presence flooding my soul with misery and desolation. My combat with

Nathan Connolly was not half as dreadful as facing this hellish demon.

I started back toward the door, but the woman creature was quicker than I. My eyes went blank, and I felt a sudden and paralyzing pain upon my shoulder. Her grim jaws pierced deep into my flesh. No words can ever describe the pain.

I accepted that these were my final moments, that I was going to collapse and would eventually awaken in the pitch dark of my grave. But then, I felt suddenly as if all of this was a dream, or I was in delirium, or even possessed. I fail to find the appropriate term for it.

I awoke in my bed, pulled aside the sleeve of my dressing gown, and there it was. A ravenous wound on my left shoulder. It hurts like death and burns as severely as hellfire.

I have washed the infected area, applied antiseptic, and taken pills, but both the agony and bewilderment is killing me slowly. I feel dizzy and restless and lie drenched in sweat, and after wrapping the laceration, I feel as thirsty as a camel despite having drained a large jug of water.

I have taken another laudanum tablet and now, I need to rest. If I am to cure myself, I must arise with a clear head at dawn.

July 4th, 1903

Jayda thinks I'm insane. I do not blame her.

I too have begun to doubt myself, for in the morning, despite the severe pain on my shoulder, I could find no trace of any wound or laceration. I saw only a slight mark upon my skin, one that settles after recovery from a deep injury.

Jayda was perplexed at first, but believes I had a nightmare, and I too share her assumption. As a doctor myself, I can see no external injury, and the pain is akin to muscle cramps.

This is how I convinced my toiling mind, which will only become at ease if Gerard ever returns.

The sooner, the better.

I feel robust after a good rest. The pain in my shoulder has vanished, and for the first time in a long while, I feel remarkably strong and determined. I feel resolute, and a stubborn rage is growing within me as the evening light fades away.

I have many things to do in a very short time. I'm prepared. Also, my longing for Gerard now fluctuates. I think this may be my final entry, for writing suddenly seems dull and lackluster.

Goodbye journal. I have better things to do.

Jayda Pearson's Diary

July 1st, 1903

It has been a long, tiresome day. I wonder how I will ever be able to find Christopher Mathers. Darryl is impatient. He says he will be leaving London to meet Sister Marion, and that I must act alone without letting anyone else become involved in the matter, and that includes Raelyn.

July 2nd, 1903

It feels like ages since the last time I prayed. Getting into the church was hard for me, for I've turned rigid after my husband's death. But I happily admit from the very depths of my soul that I left the church with a relieved heart.

Afternoon was fading and the hot glare softened into a mellow glow. I was a long distance from home, so I decided to take a cart. I was just about to duck inside the compartment when I saw a figure hurling in a state of considerable haste across the road.

A thrill of anticipation washed over me as I noticed that it was Mark Huddleston fleeing the street. I denied my ride and instead chased the frail man. His aging body, however, ran hard and fast.

I always suspected something sinister about him. There was absolutely no way that I would let him get away. There was a rage burning within me, a staunch fuming in my ears. I rushed across the lane and saw the old man climb into a cart. I did the same and commanded my driver to follow him.

After a time (and to my bewilderment), Mark Huddleston's cart stopped at our street and fled into the alley that led to Raelyn's mansion.

I chased him like a huntswoman but found no trace of him around my friend's doorstep. He had vanished. I threw my hands up in frustration and tried Raelyn's door which, as expected, was locked. I knew that she would probably be at her clinic.

Mark Huddleston must have noticed me running after him and taken shelter elsewhere. Clever indeed, but I shall not let him slip away again.

Mark my words.

July 4th, 1903

Another bizarre incident happened today. This time, it was Raelyn.

She was behaving like a frightened child, such that it gave me the impression there was a different person beneath her skin entirely, for the lovely and confident Raelyn Atherton whom I have always known never behaves in such a foolish manner.

She complained of being bitten by a savage woman with eyes like the devil. But upon looking at her shoulder, I assured her that it was nothing but a nightmare; there was a very shallow mark on her skin that reflected a slight wound, though it looked to have been inflicted upon her years ago.

I advised her to take a short leave and to rest. She is always so busy and needs to dedicate some time to her own care.

July 5th, 1903

I spent most of the day wandering the streets to find Mark Huddleston. He seems to have found some dark pit to hibernate in, for he was nowhere to be found.

I noticed a small congregation, all dressed in black, proceeding towards the cemetery. Curious as I am, I decided to join. The burial took place after the prayer and when the bells tolled, the dead man's identity came to light.

He was a sailor who spent most of his days in the arms of the sea. Those who spoke of him said he was brave and had been of valuable assistance to the British Navy. His name was Garrett Robinson. He was survived by a faithful wife named Sophie, a placid-faced woman with large, gentle eyes and grizzled hair curving down over her temples. He also left behind a brave, eleven-year-old son named Bryan, along with a significant restitution to compensate for their loss.

"He was a man of dignity," Sophie sobbed as we settled together on a bench after the burial. "He loved his profession even more than his family. Duty came before all. That's what he had always said. He meant it. And now, he can finally rest."

I checked on the boy and offered my condolences to the widow. "I do not wish to fester your wound, and I only pray for his soul to rest in peace," I said hesitantly. "Do you mind if I ask how the tragedy happened?"

"Shipwreck," she sobbed.

"My God . . ."

"It wasn't natural."

"What do you mean?" I asked.

Sophie gave me a sharp look and immediately buried her face in her palms. "He was threatened," she whispered.

"Threatened?"

"Accused of theft by a trader named Mark Huddleston. The scoundrel struck a secret deal with a rival trader but failed to keep up with the terms. Huddleston wanted my husband to bear his losses. The matter got worse as time went on. And then, this tragedy!"

"Do you believe Mark Huddleston to be involved in your husband's death?" I asked.

"God knows best," she answered at once. "But if he had the slightest hand in it, I pray that it shall never go unpunished." She broke into tears again, and I did my best to calm her down, if only for the sake of her son. She then embraced her boy and began to weep soundly. It was so distressing that I felt tears slide down my cheeks as well.

I was still consoling Sophie when Constable Barnes, whom I learned to have been a part of the investigation, approached our bench. He was a man of around forty, broad-shouldered, with curly black hair and a short, stubbled beard.

"You need to visit Scotland Yard to collect Mr. Robinson's medical reports and to leave your signature," he instructed Sophie. While he was walking away, a sudden idea made me stand and follow the constable.

"I'm Jayda Pearson," I said. "I believe I can prove to be of some assistance in your investigation."

Constable Barnes gave me a sharp look. "How?" he finally asked, knitting his eyebrows.

"I've met the man called Mark Huddleston. I know who he is."

The constable's hardened eyes watched me carefully, and then relaxed as a look of grim satisfaction spread across his face.

"Well, come along then."

July 7th, 1903

Speaking to Constable Barnes has left me awestruck, and now I feel more hatred each time I hear the name Mark Huddleston. It is only through gulping wine that I keep my agitation at bay.

"We've been unable to gather a single clue against Huddleston," Constable Barnes told me. "Justice requires evidence. I have been looking over the case for more than half a decade and have come across so many strange occurrences surrounding it. I'm afraid to admit it, but I believe there is some external force aiding Mark Huddleston."

The constable told me of a case where a man in Mark Huddleston's employ conspired with pirates to rob his master. The conspiracy was brilliantly hatched, but with a terrible consequence. The traitor met a very unnatural end. When they found his body, it was contorted beyond the limits of the human form, as if grasped and bent by the hands of the devil. His face was pale and bloodless, his body drained of it completely, his small eyes sunken deep inside his skull.

The pirates involved in the ambush against Huddleston also met their fates. None amongst them survived the shipwreck.

The navy traced the trader's ship that was destroyed in the storm to the shore of a remote island. There wasn't a sign of any person, living or dead, nor any belongings inside the gigantic vessel. Sailors did claim that they had seen a very unusual figure, something like an ape that emerged from the deck and disappeared in the mists of the island, never to be seen again.

The constable believed it was a smuggler's ship, used to illegally transport animals for trade, and that it was robbed by the pirates midway. He assumed the poor ape must have managed to avoid the pirates and fled the prison once the ship hit land.

Three other mysterious shipwrecks were reported, but again, no bodies were found, and no progress was ever made.

"The name Mark Huddleston," said the constable,

"was heard associated with each of the wrecks, and yet no evidence had been obtained."

I felt restless listening to Constable Barnes, like I had no other option but to wait and watch. However, the flame of retribution that ignited in me since Justin's death set my heart ablaze. I shared every detail I knew about Mark Huddleston in exchange for the police constable's assistance in locating Christopher Mathers.

Barnes gave his solemn word that he would help me.

"You cannot imagine how extremely necessary it is for me to resolve the case of Mark Huddleston," he said at last. "And though I'm no longer a part of the case, I will never let it go until the mystery is solved. Consider it my pride, obstinacy, or whatever other sin I possess, but my work is not yet over."

I gave a resolute smile.

"Count me in," I said.

27

Gerard Woodward's Journal

July 3rd, 1903

Ralph and I were welcomed into the arms of the devil, for Cardiff is a land of evil where betrayal resides in every soul.

It was a chilly night, a night that reminded me of my wretched stay in the castle. We were glared at in bitter hatred by each set of eyes that fell upon us until finally, we locked ourselves in our hotel room. It was the same hotel where I had first stayed during my last visit to Cardiff, though the servants had been replaced.

I no longer saw the lady at reception, Carla, nor the man who had whispered in her ear. The waiter that led me to the hall that night was also missing.

Our room was richly decorated and dimly lit, carrying with it the smell of fresh pine in the furnace, and the delightful warmth of red wine. Ralph and I were gulping our glasses when we were interrupted by a sudden knock at our door.

I answered and saw a hefty young man, dark and with a face that seemed hewn from stone, for there was not the slightest emotion upon it. He was our cart driver, the man we had summoned so that we might slip away, unnoticed by the lecherous townsfolk. Our quest was to meet with Sister Marion.

Ralph and I slipped into our cloaks, and after sharing a glass of wine with our guest, we three snuck out into the corridor.

July 4th, 1903

Ralph and I sit beside the fireplace, tending to our wounds. It brings a dreadful shiver to my spine as I recall the incident that occurred following our departure from the hotel last night:

The cart driver played his part well in engaging the woman at reception while Ralph and I snuck out the front of the hotel. We managed to sidle into the cart unnoticed and were heading at a remarkable speed towards our destination to meet with Sister Marion.

A half-moon peered through misty clouds, bathing the canopy in its silvery glimmer. The rugged track became a lonely forest road, twisting right and left until the cart suddenly came to a stop. From their perch on the driver's seat, I saw Ralph and the driver exchange a few whispered words, and the journey resumed after the driver lit a cigar.

I became absorbed in the familiar surroundings, jagged crags and rocky gorges rising from the land as we trod ever onward.

Glancing behind me, I saw Ralph and the driver exchanging sour looks. Ralph was watchful and extremely prudent, and I noticed the driver occasionally looking over his shoulder at me with a fiendish grin.

The man then halted the cart and lunged at us.

Ralph was quick enough to counter the attack, and

the two of them became involved in a nasty brawl. The cart driver tried to choke Ralph with his bare hands until I rose to my feet, raised my stick high over my head, and brought it down on the man's head.

He paused and looked at me with dull, malevolent eyes. Ralph took advantage of this mere distraction and forced him down on his back. The two of us quickly beat the man to a pulp, subduing him in the mud.

"You are the reason for our pain!" cursed the man beneath our boots, lying immobile on his back. "You were supposed to die in that castle. Instead, you killed Lady Helena! We in Cardiff are paying the price for this! You should have died in that castle, Gerard Woodward. You've ruined everything."

Ralph stiffened his weight upon our opponent's throat.

"Don't kill him, Ralph," I insisted, observing the ugly expression of revenge over his daunting face. "He shall be taken into Father Malcolm's custody."

With compressed lips, Ralph pulled the driver to his feet.

"Fate can never be overruled," the cart driver hissed. He then pulled up his sleeve and sank his teeth into a small capsule attached to his cufflink. I hurried to stop him, but it was too late. The poison was absorbed by his tongue and the poor fellow dropped dead, his eyes and mouth agape while a thick foam dripped from the corner of his mouth.

As the man died, we heard screams on the wind. Breathlessly, we ran towards the edge of a rocky lookout, and my heart sank.

The town was draped in blazing fire. We decided not to waste a moment, and both Ralph and I rushed down the track, sprinting around funnels of fire until we arrived at the convent. The structure was consumed by fire and, horribly, I saw two charred bodies nailed to the eaves.

We rushed into the house and dropped to our knees at the sight of Sister Marion hanging lifeless from the ceiling. Her face was purple and swollen, fresh blood dripping from her face, the rope tight around her neck. Ralph gave an involuntary shudder, then began to pant and weep in shock. The fire had already begun to spread its wings inside the edifice, and so we were forced to retreat.

There were bodies everywhere, though they seemed sucked dry, all skin and sinew with waxy and bloodless flesh. It must surely have been the golden-haired witch from the castle. I felt a maddening rage consume me. I was about to ask Ralph for the dagger he used to kill Helena so that I might repeat the action a second time, this time for her twin.

But I was suddenly taken aback, for at the elevated track that lay ahead of us, I noticed a large mob of enraged townspeople running towards us with torches held in hand. At first, I assumed they were our allies, sworn to avenge the deaths of their loved ones and take care of the survivors. But their foul expressions and the sudden pelting of stones at us spoke of their hazardous nature.

Ralph and I hurried in the opposite direction, which unfortunately was swallowed in flames. Seeing no way out, both my friend and I froze after saying our final prayers. It was at this moment that the great merciful God showed us a way, for tearing through the bright yellow flames rushed in a cart, driven by two wild horses and which stopped right in front of us.

"Get in," yelled a woman's voice. I was struck with awe to catch a glimpse of Carla, the previous receptionist, driving the cart. "Hurry. If they catch us, all of this will have been in vain."

I hobbled into the cart, followed by Ralph, and I do not remember anything after, as I slipped into exhaustion.

I awoke in a comfortable room furnished with oak cabinets.

The entire incident felt like a dream, which I was busy recording in my journal when the door creaked open and Carla entered with a tray of food. Ralph and I had been starving for a while now, and the three of us quickly settled at the table.

Carla confided in us that she had to quit her job at the hotel after my first escape from Mathers Castle. She voiced her opinion that I was a man of strong repute, and she was shunned for it. I'd been made a burning target here in Cardiff, and the traitors serving the Mathers very brilliantly planted the seeds of hatred into the townspeople's hearts.

Staying any longer in Cardiff was life-threatening to all three of us, so we came to the decision to leave this place.

Ralph and Carla have sided together to travel to Swindon, while I feel the urge to return to my wife. I owe her an apology. I have recently realized that I've been unfair to Raelyn, and I'm more than willing to accept any punishment for it.

London, I'm coming.

Jayda Pearson's Diary

July 10th, 1903

Sophie has begun to interact with me. I'm happy she sees a friend in me. Bryan is as naughty and as playful as a child can be, though he sometimes becomes melancholy while remembering his father. He is strong, for he has the conscience not to weep in front of his mother to abate some of her sorrow.

May the good Lord bless him.

I was late returning from Sophie's residence and had the idea of stopping by Raelyn's clinic to accompany her home. But to my amazement, her clinic was locked. I was taken by a strange feeling of unease, and I decided to pay her a visit. Upon arriving at her house, my anxiety doubled.

Her door was bolted, and so, I returned home.

July 11th, 1903

I visited Raelyn's clinic, but again, found it closed. I have started to worry. This is peculiar. The Raelyn Woodward I know never acts in such a fashion. There is a queer, acrid smell about it, something harrowing.

I wanted to see Sophie, and coincidentally, I found her in the church. Together, we mounted the spot where Raelyn and I once used to sit and gossip for hours.

Sophie had a lot of things to talk about, and she started with Bryan. Her son's aspirations worry her. She wants him to become a doctor, but he insists on following in his father's footsteps and exploring the seas. She is in absolutely no mood to give her consent.

"Bryan is the only thing I have left," she said. "I've already lost Garrett and I will not risk my son's life for a few pennies. I shall happily accept poverty over grief."

"You shouldn't be too hard on yourself," I answered. "Bryan is your son and he is young. Give him some time. He will listen to you. Hurrying things leads to nothing but misery."

She nodded thoughtfully. "You say you've seen Mark Huddleston. Where is he taking refuge these days?"

"I don't know where he stays or how he earns his living, but I can assure you that he isn't the renowned trader he once was. He is no better than a beggar."

Sophie gave a sigh of satisfaction. "He shall see worse. I pray that he rots in the street like a stray dog and there is no one to attend his funeral."

It was a few hours after noon when I returned home. I took the long route to visit Raelyn's clinic, and found it closed again. I'm left perplexed and wondering about her whereabouts. Something is not right.

I'm boiling in anger.

I cannot believe my eyes. It cannot be possible. Either

I have become insane or the world is at an end, for never in my wildest dreams could I imagine such a thing from Raelyn Woodward.

It had been so long since we last saw each other and I wanted to make sure she was all right. It was a terrible mistake. I still question what I saw, for as I entered Raelyn's street, I saw a cart pass by. There was a slight partition between the drapes, through which I astoundingly saw my friend, Raelyn, beside none other than Mark Huddleston.

The scoundrel was dressed in an overcoat and a hat, while Raelyn looked marvelous in an elegant gown, worn with a fancy hat topped with a feather of brick red. Raelyn was seated quite close to the scoundrel, as though they were a couple bound by unconditional love.

I simply cannot believe what I have seen.

I pity Gerard and I wonder what went wrong between them. Only Raelyn can clear my mind. Speaking to her tomorrow is the first thing I shall do.

July 12th, 1903

Last night was a period of little ease to my toiling mind. Morning felt as the reckoning of war, and I made no delay in rushing to Raelyn's house. Again, the door was locked. Her clinic was closed too.

I am dumbfounded. Please, God, help me through these hard times.

At dusk, I decided to break into Raelyn's house.

The garden was unkempt and the pathway across the

lawn showed that it hadn't been walked upon for quite some time. I found the spare key in the flowerpot, and I quietly entered. Raelyn's house was gloomy and dreadfully still, and a feeling of disgust overwhelmed me as I entered.

Raelyn's bedroom looked to have been recently and hurriedly ransacked; clothes lay about the floor with pockets turned inside-out, lock-fast drawers stood open, and on the hearth lay a pile of grey ashes, as though many papers had recently been burnt.

There was no sign of my friend in the bedroom or in any corner of the house, which forced me to believe she had fled.

I returned home with a sour heart.

July 14th, 1903

Two long days have passed, and my worry continues to mount for Raelyn. There is no word from Gerard either. I have written to Father Malcolm but there has been no response. Darryl has abandoned me when I need him the most.

But more than anything, I miss my Justin.

Sophie is the only one I talk to. We are bound to each other with similar pain from the loss of our husbands. The only difference is that she has a son to care for, while I'm childless and forlorn. I spent the entire day with her, we dined together, and I took it as a perfect opportunity to learn more about Mark Huddleston. But unfortunately, she had no other information left to share.

I said my farewell and was returning home when, suddenly, I saw her. It was Raelyn! She looked simply radiant, even more so than usual. She was unearthly beautiful.

To my dismay, she walked right past me, never looking at me nor speaking a word. I turned around to confront her, but she was nowhere to be found. It was so sudden and bizarre that I thought perhaps I had been hallucinating.

I still doubt my presumption, and whilst I sit at my table to write, I can only stress upon a singular thought—killing Mark Huddleston with my own hands. I swear that I shall never let that wicked man take away my best friend.

My next move shall be to visit Constable Barnes.

July 17th, 1903

The hunt for Mark Huddleston has consistently failed. He seems to have vanished into some other world ever since Constable Barnes and I joined forces. Raelyn is also nowhere to be found. Her house is deserted and left in a complete mess.

"Do not fret, dear lady," said Barnes as he stopped by my doorstep. "Huddleston is more cunning than a fox and more poisonous than a snake. Patience is what is duly required if we are to deal with a man like him."

Hearing any word about Mark Huddleston leaves me craving revenge. I shall not only bring an end to him, but I also promise to slay the Xana who took Justin from me. There is a greater purpose at work, and I need to act very cautiously. I have written another letter to Father Malcolm and hope that it shall soon be answered.

I was surprised to find Gerard Woodward at my door. He was very white and nervous. He arrived in London and came straight to me after finding no sign of his wife in their home. I did not go into detail but explained to him about Raelyn's absence from the clinic and from their home. Gerard seemed thoughtful for a moment, then immediately left.

July 20th, 1903

Gerard made another visit to my house. He was drunk, his hair and beard untidy, and his eyes red and puffy with sleeplessness and tears. Upon inviting him in, he broke into a grievous sob.

"Raelyn wants a divorce," he stammered. "How can she do this to me?"

His words stunned me too. I have no earthly idea what's wrong with her.

Gerard explained that when he returned home last night, Raelyn showed no emotion and remained silent when he told her how much he had missed her. She disappeared into the kitchen, and when Gerard asked if he could help her prepare dinner, she refused. She did not eat dinner with him, instead complaining that she didn't feel well, wanted some rest, and then retired to her bedroom.

Hoping she might feel normal after a good night's rest, he tried to wake her in the morning, but found her door locked. After knocking on it for several minutes, she ordered him to leave her alone.

"It was only after dusk that she stepped out of her room," he said. "Something about her was different; she was beautiful as ever, but there was something terrible in her beauty. I told her we were leaving for Swindon to meet Father Malcolm, and she started to scream. She said I do not own her, that she is not my slave."

Then, he told me that Raelyn demanded a divorce.

He was so confused and angry that he slapped her across the cheek (something he idly regrets), and she left the house without a word.

I tried to dilute his pain, but every time I mentioned Raelyn's name, he grunted and wept like a small child. He was not at all in a state to return home, so I allotted him a room in my house. He wanted to meet with Father Malcolm, and I assured him that we would get through these gloomy days soon enough. Though, I doubt my own words, for there can be no peace until Christopher Mathers is found and Mark Huddleston is brought before the sword of justice.

Recording this last line in my diary has struck a queer thought in mind. I'm not sure about it, but I shall leave no stone unturned.

Gerard Woodward's Journal

July 17th, 1903

I feel so relieved as my train approaches the station. I'm delighted with joy, impatient to hold my wife in my arms.

It is a beautiful spring day, with a light blue sky flecked with fleecy clouds. The sun is shining brightly, and yet there is an exhilarating nip in the air. I'm rejoicing over the thought of seeing Raelyn and fascinated by the beauty of London, which has always been such a great eminence to my soul.

I might be called a nationalist, but I'm proud of it.

———————•———————

I started home from the station, my heart racing. Time stood still, though the streets were crowded with gossip and murmurs. The cart took a final turn onto my street and at last, it stopped. I hopped out and opened the door to my home, but to my amazement, my house was empty and still. There was no sign of my wife.

"Darling," I called out. "I'm home."

There came no reply. As I moved upstairs to check our bedroom, I stopped dead on the threshold. It was a mess. Clothes and other belongings thrown here and there, furniture upended, and the drapes drawn over the windows.

It reminded me of how I found Nathan Connolly's bedroom.

I made up my mind to surprise my wife at her clinic, only to find it locked. Upon speaking with the owner of a nearby shop, I came to learn that her clinic had been closed for quite some time. His words ran like poison in my veins. It was around dusk when I reached Jayda Pearson's home, with a flickering hope of finding my wife there, but I was met with disappointment.

I returned home and met with my only companion at present— my journal. Raelyn must be out for some important purpose. I believe it. I shall wait until morning.

July 18th, 1903

The clock is about to strike noon and there is still no

sign of Raelyn. I feel like burning the entire world just to find her. I'm agitated, perplexed, and overwhelmed.

I can no longer sit meekly and wait like a crone. I need to act.

As I set out and proceeded to the church—Raelyn's preferred place to spend her spare time—I took a different route to make use of the shortcut. It was the same track that led across to Nathan's guesthouse.

I suddenly caught sight of a thin and shabbily dressed fellow in a tattered coat and baggy trousers rushing across the boundary of my wife's estate. I barked at him to stop, but he ignored me. I was about to chase him down when I heard a couple of familiar voices. I turned around and saw two of my associates, Jacobs and Joplin.

"I hope your wife took you into account with this very important decision," said Jacobs.

"What decision?" I asked.

Jacobs chuckled. "I see that you've still not given up your humorous nature, Mr. Woodward. Your dear wife, the owner of this large estate, has made up her mind to sell the property following her cousin's death."

I think my associates noticed a wave of irresolution pass over my face, for the other one immediately asked, "Aren't you aware of Nathan Connolly's death?"

I shook my head. "I have been out of town for a while and have only returned today."

I was then told about a Mr. Tanner, the man who intends to buy my wife's estate. My guess stood correct, for they told me it was the same man who had just fled the house.

"If my wife is satisfied with the deal, then who am I to interfere?" I answered after carefully examining the papers Joplin presented. "This client of yours, Mr. Tanner, seems an outsider to me. Why else would he be happily willing to pay double the price of the property? He must lack knowledge about properties in London."

"He's French," said Joplin.

I gave a nod, but I was still suspicious about this deal. Moreover, I was desperate to learn about Nathan's death and Raelyn's whereabouts. I departed for church at once but found no sign of my wife. So, I fell to my knees and prayed to God that he might make my life as it was before my doomed trip to Cardiff.

I returned home with a wounded heart. Despite my urge to visit Jayda again, I preferred a belly full of wine, after which I do not even remember falling asleep.

July 19th, 1903

I woke up late in my bed this afternoon, similar to the time I used to arise in Mathers Castle. Though now, I do not perceive much difference between the two places, for I was lonely there and I'm forlorn here as well. There was the presence of the Matherses, which terrified me, and now there is Raelyn's absence.

My body craves for a healthy meal, but I prefer wine.

After I drank three glasses, I set out on foot in search of my wife. I stopped at the cemetery and wrote to Ralph Brewer to tell him of Raelyn, and I also wrote to Father Malcom to visit me as soon as possible.

The day wasn't easy for me to endure, and after long

hours of heartbreak and desolation, I returned home after dusk. The dull sky appeared as lugubrious as my spirit, misty and blotched with heavy clouds of dismay. I wanted to cry out loud, and feeling a similar pain in my heart, I stepped into the house, unaware of the surprise that awaited me inside.

I walked into the hall and suddenly heard a kind of echo from my bedroom.

I rushed upstairs, threw open my bedroom door, and could hardly believe my eyes. There before me and seated on the bed was Raelyn, with a book and a glass of wine held in hand. As I walked in the room, I saw a light of welcome in my wife's eyes. But when recognition fell upon her face, the light faded, and she turned away with a look of disappointment.

I was baffled, but nonetheless I became entranced by her extreme beauty. Her cheeks, though considerably freckled, were flushed with an exquisite bloom. I could not help but admire her. She was bewitching.

Then a sort of memory came to me, and I felt a chill crawl down my spine.

Raelyn reminded me of someone, a woman (though not entirely a woman) whose beauty inspired fear and loathing.

Helena Mathers, may she burn in hell.

But grief and longing for my wife made every other thought fade from my mind, and I rushed to embrace her. She seemed neutral, for no emotion of joy or even regret ever came upon her, and she remained stagnant. I tried to suppress my anger and fought back my tears to speak to her. I admit that my questions must have seemed endless, but she hardly responded to any of them. Instead, she left me in the bedroom and went to the kitchen to prepare dinner. I wanted to assist her in the task, but she plainly refused.

Raelyn has changed, I fear. I have a sick feeling within me. At the very least, her temper somehow appeared normal to me, for a woman has the right to be mad at her husband when he departs so early after their marriage. I accepted my fault and sincerely apologized for it.

But things became ugly tonight, and we agreed to sleep in our separate chambers.

I wanted to take her to Father Malcolm, but she refused, and our quarrel continued. She reminded me that she wasn't my slave and insisted vigorously on a divorce, which triggered my anger to such an extent that— shamefully and for the first and only time—I hit her. The slap incensed her rage, and she left the house.

I'm in tears and cursing my actions. I need to apologize. I must. I shall do it once she returns. She deserves it.

I love her. But until then, wine is my only companion.

July 21st, 1903

My wife never returned. I doubt if she ever will. But I am no longer sad. No, I'm reddened with fury. There is something peculiar in this whole affair and I cannot sit and drink and weep. I must act.

I awoke this morning and swore to myself that I shall kill Lord Mathers and burn his castle to the ground, if need be, to get Raelyn back.

With a resolute mind as rigid as stone, I visited Jayda's house for breakfast and convinced her to disclose every single incident that had occurred here in my absence. She started with her secret meeting with Darryl, followed by Nathan's death, which took place when he broke into my house and tried to kill Raelyn. He was possessed by a Xana, which made certain things suddenly clear in my mind. Jayda claimed to have no knowledge about the sale of Raelyn's estate, for she barely walks that route. I offered her my condolences when I learned of poor Justin's death.

And then, we discussed our plan of action. It is our common cause to find Christopher Mathers, the son of Lord Mathers and the heir to his legacy. Jayda told me about Constable Barnes, who is yet another ally in our mission. She wished to be the one to bring down Lord Mathers but I begged her to stay and keep a close watch on Raelyn's estate, and to inform me whenever the sale was finalized. She also desires Raelyn to come home.

I feel a fire of vengeance within my belly. I can no longer patiently endure this torment. I've written another letter to Ralph and shall await his answer. If I am the reason for this great disaster, let me also be the one to extinguish it.

28

Jayda Pearson's Diary

July 21st, 1903

Gerard was right about one thing: Raelyn's estate is for sale. I heard two men talking about their client, one Mr. Tanner, who plans to pay double the sum to purchase it. A wise and wealthy fool, I must say. But evil has spread its wings over London and unusual actions attract suspicion. I tried talking to the agents, but they did not entertain me. I wanted to meet their client, but I was denied. So, I returned home.

As a darkening evening approached, I found that I was running out of groceries and decided to visit the market. Walking in the crowded streets has become a norm, for I'm fed up with loneliness. It scares me.

But what scares me most is dying without avenging my husband.

While returning home from the market, I thought of visiting Sophie's house, in case she needed anything. I took a shortcut that led through Raelyn's property and the guesthouse where Nathan Connolly had lived. I walked this route to fulfill my duty to Gerard, who asked me to keep an eye on the estate.

The small street was quiet, but upon crossing the boundary of the guesthouse, I noticed a shadow pass quickly across the upper window. I set aside my belongings and grabbed a pointed stone for self-defense, concealing myself in the long shade of the boundary wall. Motionless, I watched and waited for the trespasser to reveal his or her identity, but there came no other movement from inside. The place was so still that I wondered whether I had actually seen anything. But as I was about to retreat, there came a crashing sound from inside the building. Gripping the sharp stone, I rushed inside.

The first floor appeared empty and carried the smell of lime. I remained careful not to make the slightest sound and slowly ascended the stairs. I peeped into a back bedroom and found it deserted and still. There was no one, not even a footprint in the dust. But to my fortune, I saw at the corner of the chamber a broken window and a pelted stone that lay right below it. I moved closer and observed a paper wrapped around the stone. I hastily unwrapped it and stretched it upon the dusty floor.

It was a very small note, which read, *You shouldn't have killed Helena.*

The message, despite its size, conveyed a serious threat. I rushed to the window to locate the fanatic messenger but discovered no one on the grounds of the estate.

I stood by the window, staring bluntly at the grounds and dwelling on my own theories, when I noticed a pair of sharp yellow eyes suddenly glaring at me from the upper wall. I was petrified, and as soon as I stepped back from the window, it shrunk upward onto the roof and vanished.

"What are you doing here, Mrs. Pearson?" called a voice behind me, and I turned around with a drumming heart to find Gerard's associate, Jacobs, standing at the door. "You shouldn't enter someone's property uninvited. Please leave."

I pointed my quivering finger towards the direction. "There is something outside the window," I stammered.

Jacobs walked past me and peered out the window. "There is nothing at all," he grumbled.

I was stunned at his response and looked out to confirm it myself. There was nothing. Jacob had a few words with me, which I confess not to remember, for my mind buzzed with the memory of the strange creature.

I must tell Gerard. He is now the only person I trust.

July 22nd, 1903

Received a telegram early this morning from Gerard. He says he is out of town and shall return tomorrow evening. He also reminded me of my task and of finding his wife. I pity the couple. I pray for the best, though I still doubt if they shall ever be whole again.

My heart burns in acrimony whenever I think of Mark Huddleston. I cannot let my friend suffocate because of him.

With this singular thought in mind, I visited Gerard's house with the duplicate key Gerard left in my custody. A large portion of the house was clean, save for the kitchen and bedroom, which I presume Gerard avoids as they remind him of his beloved wife. I myself still struggle profoundly not to cry when I see Justin's belongings.

The wound of love, after all, is not easy to bear.

Raelyn's private chamber was gloomy and filthy. I opened the drapes to let the magnificent sunlight in, which reflected on the polished marble floor and illuminated the room.

I picked up the clothes lying all around. I opened the wardrobe, then immediately screamed and threw myself backwards upon the floor.

I struggled to my feet, paralyzed by the horrible discovery of my best friend, Raelyn Woodward. She was motionless, her skin white as milk, lips flushed with scarlet, eyes staring back at me in malice. I initially thought her to be dead, and only when I heard her shallow breathing did I realize she was very much alive.

She was asleep, with her eyes open!

I tried to wake her and called her by name, but she didn't respond. She didn't blink her eyes nor move a muscle. Just as I was about to splash a discarded jug of water in her face, she moved her head and smiled in such a way that froze the very blood in my veins. I immediately took a step back, tripped over a basket, and fell to the floor.

My eyes slightly shifted to my left, and I stared in horror at the dead body of Darryl lying beneath the bed. His features were contorted, his body fragile, his eyes fixed upward in misery. The state of his body spoke of a painful death. I felt a pain in my throat and covered my mouth with quivering hands to suppress my sobs. I crawled back to my feet, but Raelyn was no longer there. She had disappeared.

It took me a few moments to realize it was the sunlight that forced her to flee. Had I not opened the drapes, I might have been hunted down like poor Darryl. I did not possess the audacity to stay there any longer. I fled the place as quickly as I could.

A very terrible thought has come to my mind. I shouldn't have neglected Raelyn's nightmare, nor should I have concealed it from Gerard.

I need to tell him once he returns.

Letter from Ralph Brewer to Gerard Woodward

July 21, 1903
Swindon

My dear friend,

First, I would like to apologize for my delay in writing back to you. I have great news to disclose.

Sister Marion's death has outraged Father Malcolm, and he has personally traveled to Cardiff to set things right. What will delight you, my brave fellow, is the rebellion, which we witnessed with our own eyes. Carla accompanied Father Malcolm, and she informed me that the uprising has been suppressed.

Father Malcolm has fruitfully put an end to the plague of fear and has swayed them to our cause.

The people of Cardiff have become so enraged with Lord Mathers that they burnt the entire neighboring village out of retribution. This small locality was situated nearest the castle, and you will never believe what they found in the ashes. It was a land of evil, sheltering possessed men, women, and children. They were offspring of the Xana, all of whom have been eradicated. People wished to attack the castle, but Father Malcolm stopped them. He proclaimed that the evil inside the castle wants them to try and breach the gates, and that Lord Mathers and his minions are invincible in their own territory. We must find some other means to kill them.

There is another important message Carla has ordered me to pass on to you. Father Malcolm says that Lord Mathers requires fresh breeding ground for his roots of evil to spread. He has ordered you to be extremely careful in London, and to report any strange activity there with haste. I promise to be there by this coming week. Until then, you need to handle things as you always have.

Your friend always,

Ralph Brewer

Gerard Woodward's Journal

July 22nd, 1903

Constable Barnes summoned me to the station to have a talk over relevant matters.

"Do you always carry your pen and journal wherever you go?" he asked with a sarcastic frown. I chuckled and gave a nod. I felt so comfortable in our entire conversation that I not only shared the information of my missing wife, but also the details of my newest adventure in Cardiff. In response, he disclosed the strange case of Mark Huddleston.

"I think we are after the same target," I said after listening to him attentively. "Whatever clue we are chasing brings us to a similar track. My wife's estate is for sale. I believe it shall be none but this man Mark Huddleston who will show up in disguise to attain the property. I also believe that Mark Huddleston isn't who he says he is. I have a hunch, Constable, that he is misrepresenting himself. I believe he may be Christopher Mathers, the son of Lord Ferdinand Elvin Mathers."

Barnes looked shocked. "What makes you think that?" he asked.

"As I said, it is a hunch, but my experience with Lord Mathers and the news I have recently received from my friend in Cardiff may lend to my theory," I answered firmly. "I only need evidence to confirm it. I've already set Jayda for the task."

"Excellent!" exclaimed the constable. There was satisfaction upon his brows, a resolute smile on his face. "Your name is befitting of your reputation, Mr. Woodward. I see you're as keen and impatient as I am to unfold this mystery. And if evidence is what you seek, I ask you to accompany me to the scene of a new tragedy.

"It is yet another case reported at sea. What is favourable to us, however, is the presence of a witness, a fisherman who claims to have seen the entire incident. We can jump to conclusions after listening to what he has to say."

I am flooded with anticipation as we approach the port. I'm keen to conclude this entire affair, once and for all.

And as far as Raelyn is concerned, let it be known that I will never give up on my wife.

It has been only a few moments since we've returned to the constable's room in Brixton. I'm amazed and very satisfied with our visit to the port.

There remains little doubt regarding Mr. Tanner's identity. I'm quite certain that Mark Huddleston is playing the role of the client quite cunningly, and has managed to fool my associates, who I believe wouldn't have been quite a challenge for a Mathers. I have a plan, but unfortunately, it won't require the involvement of Jayda Pearson this time, for evil has its own ears and the slightest of flaws will cost us heavily.

What I'm about to disclose now is our encounter with this fisherman named Philip. He was a big, powerful chap, clean-shaven, and very swarthy.

"You must believe, good sir, that what I told you yesterday wasn't a mere fantasy of mine," Philip said as Barnes and I stepped into his boat.

"I trust you," replied the constable, then he asked the fisherman to recite his adventure again, this time to me.

Philip cleared his throat and began, "Yesterday was a rough day at sea. I could trap no fish in my usual zone and had no other option but to move beyond those boundaries. I daresay, the big blue is as dangerous as it is beautiful, and one can only realize it once he sets sail. The sun was shining overhead, and I could have sat idly by and watched the entire day if I didn't have hungry mouths waiting at home."

The fisherman then explained that an approaching vessel captured his attention on the horizon. He saw no banner on board, save for the Union Jack that made him presume it to be a trader's ship. He then noticed three other ships chasing the vessel and was certain it had to be pirates pursuing the consignment on board. They surrounded the vessel on all sides. There was no way of escape for the poor trader.

Just as the pirates were about to board, Philip explained that the trio of ships suddenly experienced a dreadful shudder, as if some invisible Kraken had emerged from the depths of the ocean. A thick layer of swirling seafoam engulfed the ships, and one after the other, they sunk deep beneath the surface. Though in bad condition, the trader's vessel managed to reach the port.

"I tailed the strange vessel to port," Philip explained, "but there was no person, living or dead, found on board. The boxes and barrels inside the hull were also empty, but ..." And here, the fisherman gulped and wiped sweat from his forehead.

"What is it?" I asked, intrigued.

"I promise that I shall never fish again, for I can never in my worst nightmares forget what I saw."

"What did you see?" I beckoned.

The fisherman gulped. "At first, I thought it to be an illusion, until the policeman appointed at the port claimed to have seen the same thing. As the vessel was nearing the port, I saw something monstrous, almost like an ape, jumping off the starboard side and into the ocean."

I felt a rush of excitement hearing those words, for what he said sparked familiarity, for I saw the same creature scaling the walls of the dreaded castle.

If my presumptions are correct, then London is in grave danger.

July 23rd, 1903

May your soul rest in peace, Darryl. May the merciful

Lord forgive all your sins and accept the sacrifices you've made in service to our cause, and to all of humanity. Amen.

Other than the servant Maverick, Darryl the cart driver is the only reason I'm still alive. The news reached Barnes this morning, and I have been flooded with questions ever since. I don't know why poor Darryl's body was found beneath my wife's bed. Jayda found it and reported it to the police.

My wife is missing, and a dead body has been found in her bedroom, though I'm convinced in my heart of hearts that Raelyn had nothing to do with it. I wanted to visit my house, but Constable Barnes says that we have other important work here in Brixton.

We're examining the tragedy at sea, and about to observe the ship's empty boxes and barrels to extract any evidence that might lead us to the truth. I appreciate the way Barnes puts immense effort into this task. It shows his desperation to find Mark Huddleston.

If my hunch to his identity proves correct, I shall lynch him myself.

Jayda Pearson's Diary

July 30th, 1903

I was chained by such grief that I couldn't step out of the house for a couple of days following Darryl's burial. His face still flashes before me, leaving me in tears.

I thoroughly fear if Raelyn had even the slightest

hand in his gruesome murder, but it did not seem wise to share this with the police, as I am hopeful for her return to London . . . and to normalcy.

This afternoon, I took the same route that led to Raelyn's estate in order to keep watch. To my shock, the estate had already been sold, furnished, and occupied by the new owner. I felt an ache of regret, as I had let Gerard down and failed miserably this singular task allotted to me. With a sickness in my heart, I walked to the door and gave a fierce knock. It eventually opened, and standing on the other side was a bizarre and grotesque old man, with a large, wrinkled face, hardened eyes, and a prominent nose that only added to his austerity.

"Mr. Tanner?" I asked.

He inclined his head, and rather than asking me in, he stepped outside and shut the door. "Who are you?"

"I'm Jayda Pearson," I answered. "A close friend of Gerard Woodward."

I noticed a spark of viciousness in his eyes, which he quite easily veiled with a smile. "Ah, the famous lawyer. I've been told that people close to him are abandoning him left and right. Is it true that his wife has disappeared?"

"Just a misunderstanding," I responded as quickly and coherently as I could, suddenly enraged at his strange remark. "I'm sure they will reconcile their differences very soon."

Speaking with him further, I failed pathetically in my efforts to convince the old man to let me inside the house. He simply gave a polite bow and disappeared behind the door. I then returned home with a hopeless heart.

I had not a word to speak to Gerard upon his return. He was in a penitent mood and seemed as if he had given up on me and would never again entrust me with anything. Though, the sudden arrival of Ralph Brewer sparked some courage within me, and I finally decided to tell Gerard of Raelyn's nightmare.

He became outraged, disgruntled, and anxious, pacing the room in a state of anger. He threw an ugly glance at me every now and then, but out of some divine light that shone within him, somehow managed to control his anger.

Ralph also had some words to say. "You shouldn't have neglected Raelyn's nightmare, Jayda," he said. "Raelyn spoke the truth of what she saw, though she mustn't have been aware of the reality of it. She has been touched by the Xana. If we do not find her and take her to Father Malcolm at once, she will become one of them. She will forever be lost."

Gerard slammed his fist against the wall.

"We do not have a second to waste," he yelled. He then ordered Ralph to visit his house and bring him the artifact Raelyn had been gifted. Ralph immediately rose to his feet and fled, then returned a short time later with an antique vase which Gerard took in his hands and observed. (Strangely, Ralph also mentioned to have found not a single onion in the house.)

"I knew it," said Gerard, a little hoarsely. "This is how they got to my wife. These enchanted pots are the vessels through which the horrible creatures move about. I have seen another in the castle. The Xana appears one moment and vanishes in another. This is where she escapes to. She travels instantaneously through these pots."

Gerard raised the vase high in his hand, and with great force, threw it upon the floor. I was expecting the object to shatter into countless pieces but astoundingly, it showed only a crack. Gerard then heaved a heavy desk and smashed the pot beneath it. This time, it shattered.

A strange stillness fell over us, as if some great danger had just escaped into our midst. The lamps flickered, and a heart-subduing silence settled in the room. None among us spoke for a long time.

It was Gerard, suddenly, who initiated our plan of action. "We will make our move tonight," he proclaimed. Constable Barnes was then summoned, and the plan of action was disclosed between us.

A wave of goosebumps erupts along my body. I'm scared. I'm nervous. I need to move and so, here I shall stop. I will clear up things eventually, if I should survive. If not, hold on, dear Justin, for your wife is on her way.

Help me, oh Lord.

Gerard Woodward's Journal

July 30th, 1903. Midnight

I am enraged, but also satisfied. I'm burning with the fire of retribution, and at the same time consumed by the flames of obstinacy. I'm broken but resolute, and I swear upon my own life, my religion, and every other thing I hold sacred that I shall not only put an end to the reign of this evil, but I will save my wife and bring her home to me.

Speaking with Jayda has cleared the recurring

clouds of doubt in my mind. I now understand the true identities of both Mark Huddleston and Mr. Tanner. Jayda's description of Huddleston reminded me of a similar figure I saw in the castle, in the corridor from inside the coffin. Now there remains not a shadow of doubt that he is Christopher Mathers, the legitimate son of Lord Ferdinand Elvin Mathers. Christopher has quite brilliantly disguised himself as Mark Huddleston in order to transport the enchanted pots around the globe and aid the Xana in their savagery. This is exactly how the Matherses found their way into London, and how they intend to expand their dark reign across the world. I promise I shall never let that happen.

And of Mr. Tanner, I've got a surprise planned for him.

July 31st, 1903

The man in the guise of Mr. Tanner is not Christopher Mathers. He is none other than Lord Ferdinand Elvin Mathers. Jayda's description of him turned my doubt into certainty.

It was late, and the red of the sky had faded into gray by the time we arrived at my wife's estate. We broke into the house from two different points: Ralph and I made our entrance through the front, while Jayda and Constable Barnes invaded from the back door. The house was dimly lit, and I heard no sound, save for our throbbing heartbeats, so acute was the silence. A book lay untouched on a mahogany table, while logs in the furnace were fresh and burning vigorously with a crackle. Ralph moved swiftly upstairs while I moved to the parlor.

And there he was.

Lord Ferdinand Elvin Mathers, sitting on an oak

chair and welcoming me with a sinister smile.

"You never disappoint, Mr. Woodward," hissed the old man. "I was expecting you here a long time ago. You're late, however, and you can do nothing. The Xana have made the right decision in transforming your beloved wife into one of them. I've never seen her happier. Mrs. Woodward will soon be feeding their infants. They shall breed and conquer every corner of this wretched globe."

I stepped further into the room.

"I pity you, Lord Mathers, for you won't live long enough to watch them fail. I shall burn your conspiracies into ashes. Trust me, Ferdinand, I've come to learn all of your secrets. You're well practiced in the dark arts and have sacrificed your wife for its cause. Helena and the other Xana aren't your daughters. You have but a son who lives under the guise of Mark Huddleston. He expands your territory under the veil of trade, possesses the power to transform himself into a dark, simian creature, and plants your enchanted pots from one corner of the world to the next."

I carefully dipped my hand into the pocket of my waistcoat and held out my handkerchief, tied in a slipknot.

"Helena met a terrible fate in Cardiff, Lord Mathers. And now, it is your turn."

A drastic change came over Mathers' face as I untied the knot of my handkerchief and scattered the pieces of the smashed pot at his feet. A demonic fury overtook him, and he rose to his feet with a poisonous stare, lunging at me with a shriek of inhuman rage and gripping his long-nailed hands over my throat.

With my free hand, I pulled out my revolver and emptied five bullets into the old man's chest. He stopped with his hands upon my neck, choking me fiercely until the reality of his demise seemed to settle in his fierce and withered eyes. His grip on my throat slackened as he dropped to his knees, then fell forward into a pool of his own blood and took his very last breath.

I coughed and gasped for breath, feeling the bruises already welling beneath the flesh of my neck as I relished the wicked old man's demise. For a moment, I forgot the other part of our plan. And then, a loud and terrible wail suddenly fell upon my ears and turned me cold and numb.

I knew that voice. I knew it all too well.

Blindly, I ran upstairs and into Raelyn's bedroom, giving a violent start and trembling at the sight of my wife, writhing like an earthworm exposed to salt. Her skin was pale and nearly translucent, her eyes a fierce and deadly yellow, glaring at me with malice, two unearthly infants cold and bloody against her bare bosom.

These were the offspring of the Xana who bit my wife. The fiendish infants had been stabbed to death by Ralph and Jayda, who watched from the corners of the chamber. The bloody, enchanted dagger was gripped firmly in one of Ralph's fists, and a hammer in the other. He had found several other enchanted vases and crumbled them to dust, just as all Father Malcolm's loyal servants, scattered across the world, had been instructed to do.

Raelyn screeched like some horrible demon and tried every way of escape. But Ralph, Jayda, and Constable Barnes quickly nailed crucifixes on each wall of the chamber. I stood upon the threshold, the singular way of escape, and watched in horror as my wife crawled like a vicious spider on her hands and feet, screeching as she lunged at me.

"Raelyn!" I yelled, unable to hold back my tears as I took in my wife's horrific state. She then paused and looked me in the eyes, and for a moment, I could have sworn she recognized me. But with a sudden burst of rage, she scuttled towards me ferociously, her teeth bared.

I then withdrew my own crucifix from my coat, a nail from my pants pocket, and the hammer from Ralph's fist. With an almighty swing, I nailed the crucifix to the floor of the doorway just as Raelyn leapt at me.

And then, Raelyn shrieked in agony and fell to the floor, paralyzed and convulsing under the influence of the crucifix. After a few ungodly minutes, she finally collapsed and went limp.

I rushed to her at once, and after placing a crucifix around her neck, we carried her out of that godforsaken place. She was unconscious for the rest of the night, and at the first light of dawn, Ralph and Jayda departed with her to Swindon. Father Malcolm would do what needed to be done to bring my wife back from the hell she'd endured for far too long.

I, however, am ordered to return to Cardiff. Christopher Mathers is no longer in London, as his true identity has been unveiled.

In the wretched land where it all began, I shall meet my final foe.

29

Gerard Woodward's Journal, Continued

August 2nd, 1903

I will be in Cardiff by morning. I've stopped at the hotel outside of town to spend the night.

Carla has joined my expedition. She's excited, not just because of our sacred cause, but also because she and my dear friend, Ralph Brewer, have agreed to join their lives together. Once the threat is conquered, they shall be married.

Congratulations, dear Ralph and Carla. May the two of you never see separation as Raelyn and I have.

———————————————◆———————————————

The fangs of death have reached the hotel. There is nowhere to hide. The war is evident. We either win and live or lose and be slaughtered.

Carla and I took different rooms adjacent to one another, situated in a wide corridor with a window at the end. It was around midnight when I retired to bed, desperate to get some sleep. I tossed and turned for hours; the thought of my wife tortured me like hell. I rolled like a caterpillar in a cocoon until, in the dead of the night, the sound of footsteps outside my door roused my attention. They came swiftly from the corridor and passed beyond my door. I sat still and silent and watched the shadow pass over the floorboards.

Steadily, I arose and looked through the keyhole but saw nothing out in the corridor. I cautiously stepped out into the passage.

At the far end of the corridor, I saw a dim light flickering, throwing feeble shadows on the opposite wall. I saw a stout man holding a candle and staring out the window. Outside, I was paralyzed at the sight of an enraged mob, now surrounding us from every corner. I recognized the man with the candle as a staff member of the hotel, addressing the large riot that had gathered outside.

Just as I was about to retreat in order to alert Carla, I watched as the man turned to face me. His face shone with fury above the flickering candle, and just as he was about to lunge at me, a door in the corridor flung open and out stepped Father Malcolm. The priest's abrupt arrival made the man with the candle stop in his tracks. His firm grip upon my shoulder made me realize that the situation was dire.

"We need to talk," he commanded, proceeding towards my room. "Your pen and paper can await."

I followed, but then turned to stare bluntly at the man with the candle, and at the large crowd outside his window.

"Do not fear that which fears me," said Father Malcolm. "They won't hurt you unless you do something stupid. Now, get inside. Let's talk."

Letter from Ralph Brewer
to Father Malcolm Isaac Simpson

August 1, 1903
Cardiff

Reverend Father Malcolm,

My heart bleeds to tell you that Jayda Pearson is dead. I still find it impossible to believe.

Per your instructions, Jayda and I departed immediately for Swindon with Raelyn in our grasp. In our cart, Raelyn had not moved a muscle, and it made me wonder whether she was still alive. But her shallow breathing comforted my toiling mind and having nothing to do at hand, I shortly fell asleep.

I have no idea how long I dozed, and only woke up at the violent shuddering of our cart upon the rugged track. I noticed Jayda awaken at the same moment, and together we noticed Raelyn lying beneath the seat. She must have fallen down whilst we were asleep. Jayda pulled her back into the seat as a loud howling of wolves fell upon our ears. I peered through the drapes and observed pitch blackness in every direction, save for the dull sky and thousands of glittering stars above.

We traversed on for a long distance until the cart came to a sudden stop and, unexpectedly, resumed its pursuit a few seconds later. Why had we stopped, only to continue? Something felt odd to me. I kept looking out at the driver, but all I saw was his back.

We moved over an elevated track, which twisted right until we came to another sudden halt. And what I saw next will forever be etched in my nightmares.

The dead body of a man fell from above the top of the cart and into the mud. Upon closer inspection, I noticed that it was our cart driver who had originally started with us from the station.

Jayda became pale, pointing at the man now in the driver's seat. He spun around and my heart fell like a stone. He was a middle-aged man, well-built, resolute, with a strong face charged with a baleful smile and eyes shining like a fiend.

It was the trader, Mark Huddleston.

Christopher Mathers.

"Welcome to Cardiff," he said with a sneer.

I quickly jumped out of the cart and glanced around at the familiar environs; a large forest at one side, an extensive plateau on the other. This certainly wasn't Swindon. I don't know what sort of hellish sorcery Mathers performed to bring us to an entirely different landscape within seconds, but here we were, in Cardiff.

My eyes darted between Mathers and the cart, where Jayda and Raelyn took shelter from this devil. I did not fear death, only feared being killed and leaving the women in the hands of Christopher Mathers.

So, I stepped forward to fight.

But suddenly, the cart flipped upside down and sent me into the mud. There stood Raelyn Woodward, yellow-eyed and abhorrent, gripping Jayda's broken neck and smiling terribly at me. I noticed the crucifix was no longer around

Raelyn's neck; I assume it must have slipped off when she fell beneath the seat. Jayda mustn't have noticed—a terrible mistake that cost her her life.

Raelyn opened her mouth and let out a horrifying screech, then lowered to her haunches as though to spring upon me. But then, we were interrupted by a flood of yells and footfalls that shook the ground. I turned and saw a large mass of townsfolk, outraged, flaming torches held high and rushing up the hill with rabid eyes set upon Raelyn and Christopher Mathers.

I watched in horror as Mathers' flesh suddenly morphed into the simian creature and fled to the edge of the plateau, jumping off and vanishing from sight. I pray that he fell to his death.

Raelyn, on the other hand, tried to dash away into the woods but was eventually intercepted and crucifixed by a religious woman, whom I was later introduced to as Sister Florence. She is presently tending to Raelyn under your command.

I conclude this letter with only a singular wish, Father. Allow me to be a part of this holy war, for I can no longer bear the agony it inflicts upon my soul. I shall not marry Carla until and unless vengeance is paid for dear Jayda. This day I stand with you and your companions. I prefer to stand with the truth.

I await further instructions.

Vengeance until my last breath.

—Ralph Brewer

Notes from Sister Florence

August 2nd, 1903

The poor, possessed woman tried to run away into the woods. With some assistance from the townsfolk, we caught her. Mrs. Woodward instantly fell limp the moment I placed the crucifix upon her neck. She was carried to the abbey and bathed in holy water.

The rashes upon her skin are worsening. She needs attention.

August 3rd, 1903

The patient sleeps during the day and awakens at night. She is changing, and her condition is unstable.

She desires not to eat from the provisions provided. She is highly repulsed by onions, so much so that her condition has worsened as a result of food poisoning. She possesses enormous strength and is entirely capable of escaping, should the crucifix ever leave her neck. Often, she tries to speak normally, as if she is Raelyn Woodward, but each time I arrive in her chamber in private, she shrieks at me to let her go.

I regret to say this, but we're slowly losing her.

August 4th, 1903

Last night made things clear, as far as the patient's condition is concerned.

The rashes on Raelyn's skin vanished when the moon came out. Her face was radiant, her lips red as a rose. She seems like a patient during the day, but just the opposite at night. She is simply lovely. She tried persuading me to let her go for an hour. Upon my refusal, however, she screamed in rage. I daresay she is horrible when provoked. The sixth of this month happens to be a new moon. I've been assigned a specific task for that date.

Until then, all we can do is to wait and pray.

August 5th, 1903

I was quite worried to find Raelyn Woodward missing from her bed this morning. She had crouched beneath the bed frame to avoid the sunlight. As I proceeded further to help her out, she thrashed at me like some venomous snake until I retreated and left her to her own devices. Eventually, she went to sleep.

I noticed the marks on her skin had reappeared, and she seems weak. I carefully lifted her back into bed and sprinkled holy water over her. But I confess it is only making her condition worsen, for despite suppressing her evil tendencies, it isn't improving her health. I also applied some holy water to the bitemark on her shoulder, but it brought about no change in the victim.

I fear she is close to death. May the angels help her.

I've received a letter from Father Malcolm. He's in Cardiff and about to strike. In his letter, he advised me to remove the crucifix from the victim's neck. I was confused and fearful at his words, but I did as I was instructed.

As expected, Mrs. Woodward broke her way out of the window and disappeared into the night. I was anxious that we might never see her again, but Father Malcolm assured us she wouldn't get very far, as the effects of the holy water have weakened her. So, I set out with two of my fellow sisters in search of her.

The night was cold and dark, the roads deserted, with a light fog sweeping across the moor. Through the bright yellow flame of my lamp piercing the mist, I noticed a cemetery situated at the end of the moor. Upon reaching the gates, I saw a slim figure dressed in crimson fabric, crouched like a hound and digging into one of the graves. It was the victim, under the influence of the dark force that has possessed her for so long.

Her savage yellow eyes were desperate for nourishment, her face pale as the fog.

The flickering light of my lamp must have distracted her, for she rose to her feet, fixing those haunting yellow eyes in my direction. A cloud passed over the crescent moon and I was left in darkness, save for the petty light from my lamp. The cloud shifted and the light returned, but the victim was nowhere in the cemetery. I was uneasy as I stood in the thickening fog, trying to perceive where she had gone.

Suddenly, she bolted through the mist with a deafening shriek. Fortunately, I was quicker than she, and held up the crucifix in my hand. She yielded.

Sisters Mary and Margaret came to my aid, and again we fixed the crucifix around her neck. They carried her back to her chamber while I entered the cemetery to have a look at the grave where she had been digging.

It was the fresh grave of a man named Morris Wilson.

The patient has become desperate for flesh and blood,

desperation that led her to the grave of a man not long dead. It chills my heart to conclude that Mrs. Woodward has acquired nearly every property of a Xana, and she may never be the woman she once was if this great evil is not dealt with.

August 6th, 1903

A new moon. The night of turmoil. Mrs. Woodward was restless the entire night. She kept waking from sleep, screaming and cursing us for chaining her to a crucifix, a symbol she loathes above all else.

She was apparently expecting some sort of assistance the whole of the night, for her gaze never strayed from the window. She shrieked and squealed in that dreadful voice, for hours on end.

It was during the final hour before dawn when her agitation reached its peak. Even with the crucifix secure around her neck, she attempted to break free and maul every single one of us. With a helping hand from every nun in the abbey, we finally got her under control. The proper verses from the Bible were recited and an exorcism was performed by Father Malcolm's assistant, after which she collapsed and did not move again.

August 7th, 1903

God is great and merciful! She has awakened!

It was around noon when Raelyn Woodward (in a sort of dreamy, vague, unconscious manner) opened her eyes, which were now colored hazel.

She remembers nothing, not a single incident in all these days, save for the initial nightmare in her bedroom in

London. She is anxious and impatient and repeatedly asks for her husband, Gerard. She is eager to learn where she is, and what is going on, and a thousand other such queries. The devilish mark on her shoulder has also vanished.

Her eyes are those of Raelyn Woodward—beautiful and hazel, affectionate and merciful; her face is glowing in a way her husband must adore. Indeed, she is Raelyn Woodward once more.

Her condition assures me that something has happened at the castle.

But what?

30

Gerard Woodward's Journal

August 4th, 1903

Father Malcolm ordered me to drop a letter to the church. On my way, I was astounded to cross paths with Ralph Brewer.

I ordered the cart to be stopped and rushed to him at once. A wave of delight ran over his face when he saw me. I was curious to learn about his presence in Cardiff. He then told me about the entire horrible incident with Christopher Mathers. My heart aches with the news of Jayda's death, and the fact that my sweet Raelyn was her killer.

Not Raelyn, no . . . the beast inside of her.

I learned that Jayda's burial had taken place in a graveyard near the abbey, and that my wife was under the care of Sister Florence.

I told Ralph that Father Malcolm was present in Cardiff. He insisted I take him to the good priest, for he had some essential information to share. Together we returned to the hotel, where another great surprise awaited my friend. I watched the relief wash over his face upon reuniting with Carla, his bride-to-be. Father Malcolm was happy to see them together again, and after a short discussion with me, decided to host a small wedding ceremony for Ralph and Carla.

"We lack time," the holy priest conceded. "We have greater things at hand, and no one knows how long he may live until the angel of death appears. Fate is unseen and delaying things is a sort of blasphemy. Hence, I proudly announce the marriage between Ralph Brewer and Carla Morrison to take place by dusk. Preparations should begin without delay."

Evening was an hour of both anticipation and anxiety. A small congregation had been invited to the hall, which was quite remarkably decorated and furnished. Candles were lit in every corner of the room, while fancy carpets sheathed the marbled floor. The place resembled a small church.

The couple said their vows and exchanged rings. As they shared their first kiss as man and wife, my gaze fell upon an old woman seated in the last row, staring at me in a most peculiar way, as if I was the reason behind her misery. Her bitter gaze reminded me of my wife.

It feels impossible to resist my urges to see Raelyn, monster or otherwise. But Father Malcolm has strictly ordered us not to leave the hotel at any cost. He has also forbidden us from sleep, for Xana can manipulate dreams. My lucid dreaming in the castle now makes perfect sense.

The 6th is the night of action.

We're about to bury the demons in their own land.

August 5th, 1903

Felt a bit slothful due to sleeplessness and wine, and had to arise early to aide in Father Malcolm's task.

We were commanded to look after the barrels of oil that would be secretly transported to the castle. It was bright morning, and we knew that the cursed Matherses wouldn't be awake to interrupt us. The labourers were instructed to misrepresent themselves as the workers of Lord Mathers, if ever his son Christopher happened to inquire as to their visit. The plan worked and our men were granted access into the castle by a servant.

I have been assured that the barrels are placed exactly as Father Malcolm has instructed. Now, we wait.

August 8th, 1903

The 6th was the darkest night of my entire life. Only now do I possess the strength to write about it.

Dark clouds over the sky had swallowed the twinkling stars while the wind blew savagely. Per Father Malcolm's orders, we coated ourselves in onion paste.

It was around an hour before midnight when Ralph, Father Malcolm, and I crossed the gate of Castle Mathers. I was struck with awe to return to the vast and towering purgatory that had nearly killed me during the early months of this year. And here I was again, back with a vengeance to bury it all beneath the face of the earth.

I listened intently to Father Malcolm's whispers about some ongoing dark ceremony in the dungeons. With good fortune, we parted ways. Father Malcolm moved into the dungeons to investigate, while Ralph and I snuck into the castle.

My companion became dazed as we attempted to navigate the maze of corridors and hatchways. To no surprise, we found many of the doors locked. Then, at last, after a thorough exploration of the entire east wing of the castle, we arrived at the chamber that, once upon a time, held me as its prisoner.

The door was unlocked. I was a little hesitant at first, but with Ralph at my side, I grew resolute and forced my way in.

There, lying in bed was the blonde twin of Helena Mathers—the Xana. Pale yet natural, radiant and bewitching as a sleeping maiden, surrounded by brightly lit candles. I noticed a line of barrels untouched across the opposite wall, content that the inhabitants of the castle seemed not to have noticed them.

At least, not yet.

A broad-shouldered man draped in a cloak and hood stood over the bed, holding what appeared to be an ancient scripture in hand. The moment Ralph moved a step closer to him, the fellow stopped his recitation and slowly turned to face us.

It was Christopher Mathers. He smiled, and then his features contorted into that of a demonic ape. He let out a ghastly roar.

I pulled out my revolver and blasted a hole into the creature's shoulder. The dreadful ape roared and threw me across the room, then leapt out the window. Without a word, Ralph bolted from the room and down the corridor to give chase.

I was left alone with the Xana.

I feared she might awaken at any instant, but the strong fragrance of onion paste upon my flesh seemed to keep her in her submissive state. I became overwhelmed with an imperious desire to end her. Firmly gripping the dagger that had slain Nathan Connolly, I stepped forward.

I raised the dagger high above my head and was about to slay the fiend when a beast leapt at me from the open window. It was a black cat with fierce yellow eyes, the same beast I had tussled with months prior. The cat scratched and hissed, and as I struggled to rip it off my face, my legs collided with a barrel. The barrel toppled, causing me to slip. I was immediately soaked from head to toe in crude oil.

I managed to scare off the cat with a blast of my revolver, but as I returned to my feet, I realized that I no longer smelled of onion paste. I now smelled only of oil.

I turned and watched in horror as the Xana slowly opened its eyes. She turned a dreadful smile upon me, and with the gentlest breath, extinguished every candle in the room. The darkness was so intense and I was so terrified that I began firing my pistol in all directions, and at once retreated from the room.

The Xana was as swift as the wind, for not only did she dodge my bullets, but she chased me like a gigantic spider on the wall, her nails as sharp as daggers as she crawled along the ceiling of the corridor. The muscles of her body stiffened as she offered me a hellish grin, staring down at me like prey.

She leapt upon me but retreated when her hand touched the metal surface of my crucifix. She screeched and disappeared in the gloom.

I scrambled towards the stairs and rushed outside to look for Ralph. A bleak cry, like an awful wail of a starving wolf fell onto my ears, turning me cold from head to toe. I was helpless in the dark, blindly pointing my revolver in every direction from which I suspected an attack might come.

The garden lying adjacent to the dungeons caught my attention, for the crystal green shimmered in the darkness. There stood the cart and our horses chewing grass on the ferny floor. The large beasts abruptly stopped eating and stared back at me. They began to snort and neigh impatiently, as if some invisible force was provoking them. At last, they became furious and began tossing their manes to and fro, rising into the air and making the cart shudder violently. I was frozen with terror as the horses broke loose from the reins and rushed at me like the hounds of hell. As they thundered closer, I saw that their eyes sparkled yellow, possessed with malevolence.

A repulsive, abominable fright grasped me upon deducing that the Xana was also capable of manipulating animals. I tried my best to outrun them, my feet slipping on the frosty grass as I headed towards the dungeons. There had come a point where I was almost beneath the horse's shoe, awaiting to be crushed like a tiny bug. But then Father Malcolm emerged from the stairs and shot one of the horses. The other stopped and reared as the thunderous sound of the bullet echoed in the night. Father Malcolm moved forward to console the animal, while I was commanded to proceed further.

The holy priest had taken care of the traitorous servants all by himself, and now it was my turn to act. When I finally descended into the dungeons, I raised my hand to my chest, but my crucifix was gone. It probably slipped off my neck while running from the horses. My revolver was gone too.

I trembled in angst and trepidation when I heard a sharp, agonizing cry.

Ralph.

I hurried in his direction and ended in a chamber with no windows or openings, save for the gigantic doorway where I stood.

And then I understood. The Xana had mimicked Ralph's voice. I was trapped.

I tried to retreat, but she was too quick and too strong. She emerged from the shadows and struck me, and I dropped like an uprooted tree. The Xana rose to her feet and threw me like a sack of rice against the hard stone wall. I tried combating the dreadful creature, but it only grew more ferocious. I was tossed into every corner of the misty room like a child's plaything. I felt my ribs break. The pain was excruciating.

I was helpless. Defeated.

Her features turned more malicious. Her dry lips, thirsty for blood, pulled back to reveal a fine layer of sharp beast-like teeth, eager to shred me to pieces. I knew it was my end. There was no longer denying it. I was happy to accept it . . .

My only wish was to meet my wife on the other side.

The Xana threw herself onto the floor and crawled at me like a terrible spider, her eyes blazing yellow. But then, I felt something familiar in my pocket that sprinkled new hope within me. Father Malcolm must have dropped it in my pocket after our little encounter in the garden.

It was the perfect time to use it.

I grinned slightly and let the Xana climb on top of me. Her cold, putrid breath was upon my face, and as she opened her jaws, I pulled out the cylindrical tube and splashed holy water into her eyes. She screeched loud enough to burst my eardrums as she writhed in pain. The water blinded her, for she thrashed her claws through the air to try and finish me off.

Father Malcolm then burst through the door, breathless and shuddering, and handed me the antique dagger.

A savage temper took hold of me as I hobbled to my flailing target. Every pain inflicted upon me and my wife by the sinful hands of the Mathers family and the Xana flashed before my eyes, igniting the fire of retribution inside my heart and maddening me with utmost fury.

I gripped the Xana by her golden hair and yanked her head upward.

"This is for my wife!" I whispered harshly, then slit open her throat. A dark, viscous fluid drained from the immense gash. She shrieked and clawed at the wound, then eventually slumped to the floor. Her body crumbled into a thousand pieces and evaporated into thin air.

I returned to Father Malcolm and noticed he was wounded. I helped him out of the dungeons and to the remaining horse, who was docile now that the Xana was dead. I told Father Malcolm to stay and rest, and not to worry about Ralph and me. Father Malcolm gave me his blessing and slumped against the horse.

Christopher Mathers was the only rival that remained.

I staggered back inside the castle and began opening the barrels. It was difficult for me to move and breathe under my broken ribs, but I had no other choice. The barrels were placed at the ends of the corridors, and after breaking the seals, I upended them all. Soon the entire place smelled entirely of crude oil.

Unable to find Ralph in any wing of the castle, I proceeded back to the dungeons. I heard the echo of gunshots down a long corridor. Through an arched walkway and up an old, dusty staircase, I entered a large hall. The immense chamber was dominated by towering pillars engraved in some ancient scripture.

Sliding quietly from pillar to pillar, I finally saw the dreadful ape, wounded in one arm but still viciously fighting against Ralph, who fired off another few rounds. I noticed a few broken pillars that had smashed the barrels beneath them, spilling black oil all over the floor. I could barely imagine the horrendous creature to be Christopher Mathers. Up close, it was dark and burly, with a broad mouth stretched open to reveal sharp teeth, bloodshot eyes enraged with fury, and claws as sharp as knives.

I wanted to join the battle, but with my broken body, I knew I would be no help. The ape grabbed Ralph in his giant palms, and while Ralph struggled to break free from his grip, there followed a tussle as they smashed from one pillar to the next. Ralph slipped free. The beast tried to tear Ralph apart with his claws, but Ralph dodged and the ape's massive strength hit the pillar, giving it a violent shudder.

Ralph looked up at the faltering ceiling, and the ape suddenly clubbed him to the ground. With a demonic fury, the beast trampled Ralph underfoot and hailed down a storm of blows until, with the last of his strength, Ralph Brewer rolled to his right and plunged a sharp object into the giant's foot.

The ape roared, staggered, and collided against a pillar with such force that a large portion of the ceiling cracked and fell heavily upon the pair of them. The beast groaned and roared and tried vigorously to slip through the rock as I rushed to pull Ralph free, but to no avail.

He was trapped.

I still remember what Ralph commanded of me then, and it breaks my heart into a thousand pieces. May this brave man be granted the highest ranks in heaven.

"Do not waste a moment, Gerard," he cried, with a note of triumph in his voice. "The rock won't hold him for long. If he slips through, you and I are finished. Our holy purpose will be in vain. Do not let your emotions fool you, Gerard. Think about your wife. Let this end here. Torch the barrel and jump out the window. Do it quickly, my friend."

"Ralph," I stammered. "I can't."

"We shall see each other in eternity. If you really care for me, return home and tell Carla how much I love her. Now, Gerard Woodward. Do it now!"

His words went like a knife through my heart. I didn't move, but simply stared at Ralph, doing my best to memorize my best friend's face one last time. The ape shifted under the rocks, and Ralph yelled at me to go.

With a bleeding heart, I retreated to the corridor and returned with a blazing torch in hand. A cold breeze brushed my face as I reached the window. As I turned around one last time, I was hit with both grief and fear, for Ralph had still not moved an inch from his spot and the ape had pulled itself from the rock, hobbling towards me ferociously.

"May the good Lord accept your sacrifice, Ralph Brewer," I murmured, and before the beast could cover the long gap, I threw the torch into the oil and jumped out the window.

A deafening blast ignited the night.

My body fell and fell until I finally hit the cold, hard water of the river. Pain and exhaustion left me floating helplessly on the river's surface, and there, I watched the castle burn like a star in the lurid sky.

I was helpless in the strong flow of the river until it carried me back to the village, where the townspeople pulled me to the bank.

This is how the dark night ended.

31

Raelyn Woodward's Journal

August 10th, 1903. Swindon

It seems as though I had been asleep for a decade, for when I awoke, the world before me had entirely changed.

The thing I loved most was waking in Gerard's arms. My husband looks hurt—both physically and emotionally. I told him about my nightmare and tried to show him the mark on my shoulder, but to my amazement, it was gone. Gerard says it was just a bad dream, one that has passed away forever. He told me that I merely came down with a terrible sickness and was unconscious for days, but I can't help thinking there is something he isn't telling me. He seems disquieted and fearful. He never speaks in detail, and I never force him to.

I am devastated to hear of Jayda's death; Gerard says my best friend died of a sudden failure of the heart. Jayda was the strongest and fiercest woman I have ever known. I knew how terribly she missed Justin. I must deduce that her grieving heart could no longer bear the separation, and perhaps that is why she has died.

I'm sad, yes, but also delighted to think about their eternal reunion in heaven.

May their beautiful souls be showered with blessings.

August 20th, 1903

My husband and I have returned to our home in London, and Gerard has bought back my family's estate. He is so happy, and I am more satisfied than ever. This is the life I have always dreamt of.

My husband is so delighted to learn of my pregnancy. Our child shall grow in the service of Father Malcolm Isaac Simpson. May the good priest recover quickly.

Gerard says we shall also legally acquire Jayda's property so that no one can take away my best friend's home. Nothing is a better reward for me than that. Jayda Pearson and I were, and always will be, friends forever. She left me a little early in this mortal world, but I believe we shall be reunited in the clouds. I await that day.

Hard days have passed. I pray that they shall never return.

———————◆———————

Gerard Woodward's Journal

August 10th, 1903

All praises and thanks be to you, oh Lord! Life has returned to normal, to what I have always dreamt of.

My wife and I spend a lot of quality time together. She hardly leaves my side. Raelyn has recovered, while the mark on her shoulder has also vanished. Father Malcolm has assured me that Raelyn is fine. He also seems to be making a rapid recovery himself. God bless the holy man.

Raelyn seems satisfied with my explanations. I do not have the heart to tell her every detail. She will continue to grieve and pray for Jayda, but she must never know exactly how Jayda died. She wouldn't be able to bear it. She has already bore so much, and I won't let her suffer any longer.

This journal will forever be preserved in my records. Perhaps someday, it may prove a great source of adventure for some faraway reader. I will die happily knowing that my efforts and my sacrifices shall never go in vain.

All bad memories shall fade in time.

ABOUT THE AUTHOR

Lucas Hault is a Gothic horror novelist residing in Ranchi, India. He received his formal education and graduated from Jamia Millia Islamia. *The Malign: A Collection of 12 Short Stories*, also by Johar/Hault, was published in 2021. His first novel, *The Shadow of Death: The Conquering Darkness*, was published in 2018 by Prowess Publishing. He is also a screenwriter and has written a number of short horror films. To learn more about the author, visit www.lucashault.com.

CONNECT WITH LUCAS HAULT

Sign up for Lucas' newsletter at
www.lucashault.com/newsletter

To find out more information visit his website:
www.lucashault.com

Facebook:
www. facebook.com/lucas.hault.792

Instagram:
www.instagram.com/lucashault33

Twitter:
www.twitter.com/lucashault

BOOK DISCOUNTS AND SPECIAL DEALS

Made in the USA
Middletown, DE
25 February 2022

61831600R00149